Praise for *Dogs Don't Break Hearts*

"An impactful story about taking accountability, the perils of letting others control your narrative and, most importantly, the healing power of dogs. Dogs may not break hearts, but this book mended mine."

— Kristopher Mielke, author of *Losing Hit Points* and *Lonely in Happy Town*

"This heartfelt story crackles with authenticity and sparkles with joy. The characters are people you want to be friends with, the feelings are utterly familiar to anyone who has ever felt like they've messed up everything, and the message is one of acceptance and celebration. Plus, it has dogs, and dogs make everything better."

— Michael Thomas Ford, author of *Suicide Notes* and *Every Star That Falls*

"*Dogs Don't Break Hearts* is for anyone who has had their own heart broken, anyone who roots for the underdog, or anyone who has found love in a cold nose and a warm heart. Readers will commiserate and cheer for Beck after his relationship goes to the dogs and he stumbles into a second chance alongside some rescue canine counterparts. Two opposable thumbs up from this human and four dewclaws up from my pups."

— Paul Coccia, coauthor of *On the Line* and author of *Leon Levels Up* and *Recommended Reading*

Praise for *Stuck With You* by 'Nathan Burgoine

"Hilarious and an all-around enjoyable read... Highly recommended for hi-lo readers who loved *Heartstopper.*"

— ★starred review, *School Library Journal*

"Two charming leads readers can't help but root for... An adorable romance with strong coming-of-age elements."

— *Kirkus Reviews*

"*Stuck With You*, part of the Real Love series, is a well-written and believable narrative that addresses the many struggles people who identify as LGBTQ+ may face. Although most of the story takes place within the confines of two seats on a train, Burgoine does a solid job of using that singular setting to introduce complex issues including gender fluidity, not knowing what to do after high school graduation, navigating changing friendships and relationships, and the difficulties of dealing with shared custody."

— *CM: Review of Materials*

Dogs Don't Break Hearts

Dogs Don't Break Hearts

'NATHAN BURGOINE

JAMES LORIMER & COMPANY LTD., PUBLISHERS
TORONTO

Published in Canada in 2025. Published in the United States in 2025.

James Lorimer & Company Ltd., Publishers acknowledges funding support from the Ontario Arts Council (OAC), an agency of the Government of Ontario. We acknowledge the support of the Canada Council for the Arts. This project has been made possible in part by the Government of Canada and with the support of Ontario Creates.

Cover design: Tyler Cleroux
Cover image: Shutterstock

Library and Archives Canada Cataloguing in Publication

Title: Dogs don't break hearts / 'Nathan Burgoine.
Other titles: Dogs do not break hearts
Names: Burgoine, 'Nathan, author
Series: RealLove.
Description: Series statement: Real love
Identifiers: Canadiana (print) 20240514637 | Canadiana (ebook) 20240514653 | ISBN 9781459420076 (hardcover) | ISBN 9781459420069 (softcover) | ISBN 9781459420083 (EPUB)
Subjects: LCGFT: Romance fiction. | LCGFT: Novels.
Classification: LCC PS8603.U73713 D64 2025 | DDC jC813/.6—dc23

Published by:
James Lorimer &
Company Ltd., Publishers
117 Peter Street, Suite 304
Toronto, ON, Canada
M5V 0M3
www.lorimer.ca

Distributed in Canada by:
Formac Lorimer Books
5502 Atlantic Street
Halifax, NS, Canada
B3H 1G4
www.formaclorimerbooks.ca

Distributed in the US by:
Lerner Publisher Services
241 1st Ave. N.
Minneapolis, MN, USA
55401
www.lernerbooks.com

Printed and bound in Canada

For Chopper, Coach, Bailey, Buckley, and Delilah —

and all the other puppers. Even you, Max.

01 Today's Gay Agenda: Volunteer

GOING THROUGH A DOOR shouldn't be hard. A door I've gone through countless times should be even easier, right?

That's what I kept telling myself, over and over. Two weeks into my last year of high school, and I'm staring at the yellow door decorated with all the rainbow flags like it's grade nine and I've never been there before.

Back then, it took me days to work up the courage.

Okay, fine, weeks. I figured I'd throw up when I went in.

I didn't. Throw up, I mean. Did go through the door. Didn't throw up. Instead, I met a bunch of people who really got me. The people behind the door turned grade nine into one of the best years of my life.

Now, three years later, they were my friends. People I counted on when things got overwhelming. Who I went to when my world got screwed up.

Like now.

My world? Definitely screwed up. Problem was, one person behind that door was the whole reason.

Which meant I *couldn't* go in there. In fact, maybe I couldn't go in there ever again, which freaked me the hell out. My friends might be in there, but Mason could be, too.

Maybe he hadn't gotten here yet. But even if he wasn't already at the GSA, there was no way he hadn't told everyone.

For the first time ever, I wished a pride flag didn't cover the door's little window. I could look through to make sure Mason wasn't there.

He probably wasn't.

I mean, I'd come straight after the bell. I still had my physics books. I'd only stopped at my locker to grab my phone, then booked it for GSA, saw the door, and . . .

I'd kind of *stopped*.

I waited at the far end of the hall, by the corner. The thought of taking another step was too much.

Totally grade nine all over again.

I lifted my phone and aimed the camera, framing the door to one side and zooming out. It made the door look *really* far away. I took the picture. Perfect for today's photo. Super depressing, but really capturing my day.

I usually loved that door.

I hated it right now.

I wanted my friends. Especially Nico. But I really didn't want to see Mason. He'd definitely be coming, too. That's how it worked. We're a group.

Then it hit me.

I didn't know if that was still true. We had been a group, sure, but now?

I wasn't sure now, because when it came down to it, my friends weren't just *my* friends. They were *our* friends. And . . .

What if they weren't? What if I'd made such an ass out of myself that this was when *our* friends would become *Mason's* friends?

Maybe they already were. I'm not Mr. Outgoing. My mom says I'm like my dad: I talk like every word costs money. I prefer watching. I like listening to people, especially funny, outgoing people like . . .

Mason.

Fuck. Why had I been such an idiot?

How had I been such an idiot?

Okay. Assuming Mason wasn't there yet, would it be better if I got there first? I could sit down, find something to do. Talk to Nico or A.J. and not look at Mason when he showed. I could handle that, right? I could work on photos, or flip through my physics textbook, or . . .

Or something. Anything. I couldn't walk in and have everyone stare — that I for sure couldn't handle — and I was running out of time if I didn't just *cross the hall* and *go inside.*

I didn't move.

Then it was too late. Mason came through the doors at the other side of the hallway, heading right for the GSA door, with Maya and Amélie.

I ducked back behind the corner.

Mason was talking. I couldn't make out any words, but I knew his voice. Maya and Amélie answered. They weren't whispering, exactly, but definitely making sure no one could hear them.

I risked looking around the corner. Mason wore his favourite blue shirt and dark jeans combo. He gestured while he talked, so he was telling them a story. He always talked with his hands.

Mason looked great. He always did when he wore that shirt. It made you notice his grey eyes, and it fit him really well. Tight in a good way.

This is so unfair.

I'd chosen my oversized grey hoodie. I'd used more hair gunk than usual to defeat my bedhead, and my eyes were puffy.

I didn't think Mason's eyes were puffy.

Maya laughed at whatever Mason said. Amélie kept nodding and saying, "Oh." That much I could make out.

I ducked back behind the corner.

Was Mason telling Maya and Amélie about me? About "letting me down easy" and explaining what we "really were"?

God, I hoped not, but what else could it be? I still couldn't hear what he was saying, but he didn't sound upset.

Mason, Maya, and Amélie came into view again, and all three of them paused at the door. I hid like a coward, listening. In case someone came from the other direction, I pretended to be interested in the display on the cork board wall outside the office.

Big green letters said: *Don't Forget Your Volunteer Hours!*

"It'll be fine," Maya said.

"Yeah. Okay," Mason said. If Maya was comforting Mason, maybe Mason wasn't completely fine. Had he told them?

And what had he said?

"Come on," Amélie said.

Yeah, they were definitely comforting him. Which meant Maya and Amélie knew. Which meant *everyone* knew already, or they'd learn about it in a few minutes when the meeting started. Or by text, now that school was over and we could all use our phones again.

God, I could only imagine the texts. *Did you hear about Beck*? Five words didn't seem like much. Or would it be *Beck and Mason*? Not that there was a Beck and Mason. Not any more.

No. Not ever.

That was the worst part.

We *weren't* broken up. Because as far as Mason was concerned, we'd *never been dating*. Somehow I'd been dumb enough not to know that. I'd thought he was my boyfriend right up until I'd seen a text on his phone from another guy, and —

I heard the door open. I caught more voices from inside the room, including Nico. I really wanted to talk to Nico.

The door closed, cutting off all their voices.

Too late.

I stared hard at the notice board. It listed off all the requirements for claiming our volunteer hours. Forty hours total, or you couldn't graduate. It made no sense to me.

For one thing, if they force us how is it volunteering?

My parents hadn't agreed when I pointed that out. Or, well, they had — my dad especially — but they wanted me to graduate, so it didn't really matter. Forcing volunteering wasn't volunteering but it was still a box I had to check off if I wanted to graduate.

Life is full of stuff you have to do, my dad had said. *Sorry, bud.*

I shoved my hands into my hoodie pockets and stared at the notice like it was the most interesting thing ever. I have no idea how long I stood there before my phone vibrated.

You coming, B? The message from Nico reminded me I couldn't stand here forever. But I didn't have an answer.

No, that wasn't true.

Mason looked great. Comfort from Maya and Amélie or not, Mason *always* looked great.

I did not. I felt like crap and looked like crap.

I tapped a reply: No.

Once I sent it, I felt better and worse at the same time. Better because walking into the GSA right now? Way too hard. Worse because I really wanted to see my friends, but Mason was in there, too.

You sure? We're choosing the volunteer thing. Nico's reply came with a bored eye-roll emoji.

I groaned. Of course that was today. I glared at the board outside the office. Volunteer hours. Over the summer on our group text, Mason came up with us all volunteering at one place. Doing it as a group would be fun.

He also thought something queer-related would look great for applications, which was probably true.

We were supposed to bring our ideas to this GSA meeting. I hadn't come up with any, because Mason wanted to volunteer at Bruce House, and he'd asked me to vote for that, too. Bruce House helped HIV-positive people find places to live, as well as helping them with a bunch of different needs through volunteers.

He hadn't had to convince me. It sounded like a great way to help people and it was queer people in Ottawa. I was a little scared of trying to help strangers at all, let alone strangers who needed me not to mess up, but Mason pointed out that if we'd get to do it together as a group it wouldn't be anywhere near as scary. They wouldn't make a bunch of teenagers do anything really important.

That last part was probably the biggest relief. From the website, it looked like mostly we'd deliver food, or man phones, or stuff like that.

Either way, Bruce House made earning volunteer hours seem less bad.

It'll be easy! Mason had said, which I wasn't sure was true, but at least Bruce House would be somewhere no one was going to question us. Nico wouldn't even have to worry about his nail polish, and A.J. could wear whatever they wanted. We'd be ourselves.

Except now there was no "ourselves." No Mason and Beck. If the rest of the group agreed with Mason's idea, they'd all volunteer at Bruce House together.

Would Oliver be there? The text I'd seen on Mason's phone from Oliver, along with the very shirtless picture of Oliver, flashed in my head. I'd recognized him from last year, at the multi-school Pride Prom. He'd gone to another school, a year ahead of us.

Probably he'd be in university now. He didn't need volunteer hours. I did.

I closed my eyes. This was the worst.

My phone vibrated.

Beck? Hello???

I swallowed, then typed a reply.

Skipping the meeting. I knew Nico wouldn't be

satisfied with that. I thought about it, and added, **Stuff to do**. There. A lie, but better than "I don't want to see Mason happy when I'm a wreck."

I sent the message and waited. It didn't take long for Nico to reply.

Giving Mason space maybe isn't a bad idea.

I almost laughed. Giving *him* space? What did *that* mean? But before I could even try to reply, another message appeared.

What about volunteering?

I stared at the second message for a long time. I knew what Nico meant. Giving Mason space meant not being around any of them. They were choosing to do something together.

I've got something, I wrote back. Also not true, but if any of this got back to Mason, I didn't want to look completely pathetic.

It occurred to me they could all be watching this conversation, but I didn't think Nico would do that.

You do? What?

And of course Nico wanted to know.

Okay. I needed a plan. Right now. I looked at the Volunteer Board, and my eyes caught on the word "rescue." I definitely needed to be rescued. I went to the poster. The office put together dozens for students looking for ideas for their volunteer hours, from organizations looking for volunteers.

Rescues in Motion. There was a picture of a pretty Black woman holding a brown and white puppy beneath the title, and beside her, more words: *Every week, Rescues in Motion rescues animals from shelters, often from the euthanasia list. We need volunteers to help with the dogs, from cleaning up after them (yes, we mean dog poop!) to giving them exercise (walking on leash!) and stimulation (playing and training!), as well as drivers and people willing to provide temporary rescue homes.*

Perfect.

At the bottom of the poster there was a website and an email. I took a picture of it with my phone, then swapped back to my messages from Nico.

I'm going to help dogs. I hit send before I could change my mind.

Nico started replying with dog and bone emojis, one after the other. I laughed and sent back a thumbs-up, even though it didn't stop him.

I re-read the poster, but it didn't look like there was any deadline. Hopefully, I wasn't too late to volunteer with them. I glanced at the GSA door. Nico was in there. So were Maya, Amélie, A.J., and grade nine, ten, and eleven queer kids, who'd kept arriving while I stood there.

And Mason.

Nope. Not today. I could not.

I turned and walked away, leaving the yellow door, rainbow flags, my friends, and not-even-an-ex-boyfriend Mason behind me.

Compared to Mason, dogs would be great.

For one thing, dogs don't break hearts.

02 Today's Gay Agenda: Walk Through a Door

ZERO SURPRISE Mom didn't forget today we were planning the volunteering stuff. The moment I got home, she leaned out from the kitchen and said, "How'd it go? Did you pick something?"

She'd had the day off, which explained the smell of food cooking in the kitchen. On Mom's days off, we cooked a bunch of stuff to put into the fridge and freezer for the week ahead. It smelled like she'd gotten a head start without me, which probably meant she had plans tonight.

She stood there looking at me once I got my shoes off, and I remembered she'd asked me about my volunteer hours.

Right. That.

"Uh." I hung up my jacket. Mom sort of *flinched*. A line shows up between her eyebrows when she's stressed or worried, and it was back. I hated how often it showed up these days. A lot of it was her job, but right now? Pretty sure I'd done it.

"Timmy," she said, and now it was my turn to flinch, because *everyone* called me Beck except my parents, who stuck with Tim or — if they were doing the *I'm worried about you* thing — Timmy. I hated being called Timmy. "You have to have volunteer hours to graduate."

"I know." I did know. I tried not to sound too frustrated. I mean, I had the entire year to do it and it was literally September, but it really bugged her. She didn't put things off. She liked lists, and finishing lists.

She made lists for me, and Dad when he was home. I usually didn't mind.

This would bother her.

I needed to fess up.

"I've found something," I said. "But I have to apply first. If they accept me, I'll be good."

"Oh." She smiled like I'd solved world hunger or something. "Great. What did you all decide on?"

"I'm doing something on my own," I said.

Her eyebrow line came back. "Oh?"

"I'm not doing the group thing. I'm going to help at an animal rescue place. Dogs." I slid past her into the kitchen and checked the fridge for something to drink. As always, zero pop; only milk and orange juice. There was never any pop until Dad was home, and he was halfway across the country right now in his truck. I grabbed the milk and poured a glass.

"You know you can't bring a dog home, right?" Mom said. "Your dad is allergic and no one is home most of the time."

"I know," I said, and okay, it came out with a bit

of attitude.

Or maybe a lot of attitude.

My mom crossed her arms.

"Sorry," I said. "Rough day. I didn't mean to snap." She said that to me when she got cranky. My mom managed a chain bookstore, which is honestly pretty cool, but COVID messed up her job. Sales *tanked* when everything closed, and after they opened again, her staff got cut way back. She worked every weekend now, both days. With fewer people going downtown, she didn't have as many customers.

I knew Mom and Dad worried her head office would close the store when their lease was up. She might not get moved somewhere else. It'd just be "see ya!"

"What happened?" she said.

Did any guys talk to their moms when they broke up with their boyfriends? I doubted it.

Also? Mason *hadn't* been my boyfriend.

"Is it okay if we don't talk about it?" I said. My mom was huge on consent and privacy and stuff. I didn't ask for privacy often. Not unless it mattered.

She exhaled. "Should I be worried?"

If I didn't say something, she'd probably push.

"It's just friend stuff." Technically not a lie. Mason said we'd been *friends*. Pretty sure he didn't want to be friends now, but still.

Also, other than a couple of messages from Nico, no one else had even texted today. The Mason thing blowing up in my face sucked because Mason hung out with the same people I did. There were only so many out queer kids at school.

I basically had six friends. Emphasis on *had*.

Probably should have thought of that before sleeping with him.

Yeah, "friend stuff" covered the whole disaster.

"Okay." Mom raised her hands for a hug. I rolled my eyes, but I didn't mind. She gave me a big hug. I squeezed her back.

"I'll drop it," she said. "Love you."

"Thank you." I only squirmed a little.

She squeezed me again. "A-hem."

"Love you, too," I said.

"Good." She finally let go. "Why don't you go do the application for the dog thing right now," she said. "Check it off your list, then help me with this." She gestured to the kitchen counter. Ground beef, tomato sauce, and a bunch of vegetables. Chili or pasta sauce, looked like. Our two giant crock pots sat on the counter, so probably both.

Like I said, Mom believes in prepping things ahead of time. She wasn't kidding about checking something off my list. I hadn't made a list today, and if I had, I would have forgotten to put volunteering on it, but whatever.

"Okay," I said, and went to my laptop in my room.

Rescues in Motion's online volunteer interest form wasn't long. I had to make a profile, check one box because I was under eighteen, and another box asking if I wanted volunteer hours for high school.

Yes. Yes, I did.

They had stuff I'd have to read, I'd get on-site

training, and I liked the sound of "No form of harassment or discrimination will be tolerated." When I was done, I took a few seconds to explore the website.

Okay, fine. I looked at dog photos.

Whoever took their photos needed to up their game, though. Like, if the goal was to make you want these dogs, the photos failed. Dog after dog looked at the camera in their kennels. They looked sad, which I guess might get people to want to make them happier, but even the puppies looked miserable.

Maybe I didn't understand. But I wanted to fix it, especially after I read the write-ups on the dogs, which were actually really funny.

Oscar the Wonder-Schnauzer is here for your love and to eat your shoes. He's a little scared around other dogs, but he'll snuggle in your lap for hours if you tire him out first. He's three years old, up to date on all his shots, and looks dapper in a hat. But we're serious about the shoes.

I laughed. The dog in the picture was definitely a schnauzer, but he was just sitting on a dog bed and looking at the camera. Why tell me he looked good in a hat if you weren't going to put a hat on him? Or give the little fuzzy dog a shoe, maybe. *Something.*

Too bad. I bet Rescues in Motion wouldn't have to wait long to find a home for Oscar if they gave him a hat.

The website also had an events link. Turned out they took dogs to park festivals and stuff. They'd done Ottawa Pride last year. They had pictures from Toronto Pride and Montreal Pride, too.

The dogs even wore pride flag collars.

That had to be a really good sign. Also, the event photos were better. The dogs looked happy in them, for one.

Then again, I would also probably be happier if I, like the golden lab puppy in one photo, was being kissed on the forehead by a hot shirtless dude in a rainbow flag kilt.

Rescues in Motion's front page said they had a big need for towels and blankets right now.

When I went back to the kitchen, I turned on the tap and washed up.

"Do we have extra towels and blankets we don't need?" I asked. "Rescues in Motion wants them." I dried my hands and Mom slid over a cutting board and some tomatoes.

"Dice those," Mom said. I started cutting. She chopped a red pepper, then stopped, thinking about it. "We definitely have towels. Do you think they care if they're stained? They're your dad's." She gave me a little grin. I knew what she meant.

"They're for dogs." I didn't think stains would matter. My dad was a long-haul truck driver. He definitely went through towels. Also shirts and jeans. And oh my God, his *socks*. Dad got dirty just existing, actually. Mom threatens to make him hose off in the garage sometimes, but I don't think she means it.

"We can check after we get everything into the crockpots," Mom said.

After we were done with the pasta sauce and chili, we found a whole bunch of towels, and we had some of the casserole my mom had already put in the oven for dinner.

"You okay if I head out after reading time?" Mom asked, once we were done eating.

"Sure." I loaded the dishwasher and we went into the living room for reading time. Having a mom who manages a bookstore means two things: One, there are always books around, which I love. And two, she makes us sit and read after every dinner for an hour, every night, without fail. I didn't always love that as much, but even my dad isn't allowed to skip it when he's home, so I know better than to complain even if there's something else I want to do.

She didn't care if most of what I read was graphic novels, either.

Mason thought it was really weird the first time my mom told him he could pick any book he'd like or bring one of his own, but I'd liked sitting on the couch with him, reading together.

Not that we'd be doing that again.

I heard my phone vibrate in the kitchen but another rule of reading time? No phones. I didn't get the message from Nico until an hour later.

We're all volunteering at Bruce House, Nico said. That was it. I couldn't think of a way to respond.

I mean, what could I say? *Have fun hanging out with everyone but me?*

"You okay, honey?" my mom said. She'd changed, but she hadn't gotten dressed up or anything, so I figured she was hanging out at a friend's house. Sometimes her friends came here, and I'd go to my room because they mostly drank wine, laughed, and watched the *worst* movies.

"Sure," I said. Total lie, and I think we both knew it. But I took a breath and forced a smile. "It's okay." This time it came out better, but she didn't leave. The line was back between her eyebrows, too.

"I'm really looking forward to helping the dogs," I said. At least that felt more like the truth.

It worked, and she left.

I picked up my phone and re-read Nico's text. I still had no idea what to say.

I did my homework, had a shower, then scrolled through the photos I'd taken today, looking for something for "Today's Gay Agenda."

Choosing something for my photo stream wrapped up my day. It usually made me feel better. Some days it felt more important than others.

Today it felt important.

I found the photo of the GSA door. I usually didn't upload photos that could lead back to me, but the more I looked, the more I wanted to choose it for the feed. I'd never shown my Today's Gay Agenda feed to anyone — not even Mason — so it wasn't likely anyone would figure out who I was. Not like anyone cared, to be honest, though Today's Gay Agenda did technically have more followers than I did.

Besides, it was *just* a door.

I fiddled with the photo, using different crops until the door looked far, far away. I nudged the colour almost all the way down to black-and-white, but not quite. With the rainbows on the GSA sign, the colourful posters, and the bright yellow of the door itself, it wasn't right. But drained to something almost colourless?

Yeah. That suited my day. I uploaded it and wrote **Today's Gay Agenda: Walk Through a Door.**

My last two pictures had gotten some likes and comments, but I didn't feel up for reading them. I knew better than to check screened comments if I wasn't in a solid mood. Sometimes I got trolls, *especially* anti-trans assholes when I dared to mention trans or nonbinary people at all.

I so wasn't up for trolls today.

The comments could stay hidden. I'd unscreen the good ones later.

Instead, I explored the Rescues in Motion website again until it was time to go to bed. Cute dogs, but picture after picture of dog faces in kennels, usually centred and boring?

Their photos really sucked.

03 Today's Gay Agenda: Don't Get Parasites

THE NEXT MORNING, I got an email from Rescues in Motion saying they could do my orientation on Thursday after school. I'd heard from Nico that they were all getting trained after school on Wednesday and Thursday at Bruce House, and doing their first placement on Friday, so it meant the entire rest of the week I wouldn't see anyone from the GSA.

I couldn't decide how I felt about it.

Other than relief, I mean.

People knew *something*. I heard a few whispers, definitely noticed people looking at me, and did my best to keep my head down. This semester, I didn't have any classes with Nico, but I did see Amélie in Physics. She sort of *nodded* at me, all awkward and cold. I didn't really linger or try to talk to her, and she sat two rows over anyway, with her basketball team friends, so we never chatted much in class to begin with.

When class ended, she left without talking to me, which definitely didn't feel like a good sign. She and Mason had always been tight. They were both really outgoing, and funny. Amélie always made me laugh when she told stories, but I doubted I'd be hearing her stories any time soon.

By the time I packed up my stuff at the end of the day on Thursday, I really couldn't wait to leave.

My first trip to Rescues in Motion wasn't bad. I didn't have to take the train, just one bus, and when I got there, the building itself seemed okay. It honestly looked like a small strip-mall until you saw the yard.

So many chain link fences went around the edge of the property, even across the driveway. The ways in and out all had two sets of gates. As I walked up, I heard faint barking from inside.

I'd brought about half the towels my mom and I had found in my backpack, and was fifteen minutes early. I went through the front door and it chimed, but no one was in the room.

I unzipped my backpack and pulled out the towels.

Doors opened behind the desk in the little entrance area, and a tall, skinny white guy came through. He didn't look as old as my mom, even, but his black hair already had streaks of grey. He wore jeans, a red polo shirt, and a white smock.

Dude got really smiley when he saw the towels. I've never seen someone actually *excited* about towels before. He came right around the desk to take them from me.

"Are all those for us?" he asked.

"Yeah," I said. "Your website said you needed them?"

"Endlessly. Thank you." He tucked them into a big basket beside the desk.

"We washed them," I said. "I know they're stained, but my mom says they're still good, just, y'know, stained."

"Stains are fine. But we have to wash them again," the guy said, with a big grin that showed off his teeth. "Nothing personal, just the rules."

"Okay." I nodded. "I have more, but that's all I could fit."

"That's great!" He kept looking at me, like he was maybe confused why I hadn't left now that I'd dropped off the towels.

"I'm Tim Beck," I said.

"Oh! Right!" he said, laughing. The guy did not seem to do anything without smiling, grinning, or laughing. "Timothy Beck, Central High, volunteering." I'd swear he was repeating something he'd memorized. "You're early."

"That's me." Would he tell me *his* name? He wasn't awkward, exactly, but he reminded me of something A.J. said about their older brother, Dominic: *Dominic doesn't do people very well.* Maybe this guy was the same, and needed extra social cues? I held out my hand. "Everyone calls me Beck."

"Okay. Beck." He repeated it. "I'm Jonas. I'm one of the vet techs. I don't usually man the front." He laughed again, and I thought maybe he was nervous. "That's probably obvious."

"It's okay," I said, because I felt like I should say something. I didn't love talking to strangers either. I wouldn't want to man the front desk. I definitely wouldn't want to answer the phone.

I hoped phones weren't one of my volunteer jobs.

Jonas clapped his hands together. "Let me find Heather. She'll give you the basic tour, and we can talk parasites."

I blinked. Did he really just say that? "Parasites?"

"Parasites." He laughed again. "You'll be scooping a lot of poop, Beck, and we have to be careful. Gloves, boots, poop scoops . . ." He spread his hands, still grinning. "Parasites are bad. We don't want parasites."

"Right." I really didn't. *Parasites*? I thought I was here to look after dogs.

"Oh God, Jonas, stop," someone else said, and I turned.

A girl closer to my age, but still a couple of years older than me, had come through the door.

I totally stared.

Her dark brown hair was shaved on one side of her head almost to the scalp, but on the other side it was long and dyed dark purple at the tips. What really caught me though was her makeup game. Around her left eye she'd extended intense black and purple eyeliner into curls and spikes.

She looked *awesome*. Butch but also femme, if that was possible.

"This is Heather," Jonas said, still grinning like a goofball. "She'll be giving you your orientation. Heather, this is Timothy Beck." He turned to her. "Don't forget parasites."

"I swear I won't forget the parasites." Heather shook her head, then smiled at me. "Come on, *Timothy*

Beck." The way she said my name was funny — she'd done a pretty spot-on impersonation of Jonas's over-the-top happy voice.

"Everyone calls me Beck," I said. I followed her through the door she'd come in through, into a short hallway. At one end, behind a big pair of double doors with frosted glass, I heard a few dogs barking.

"Beck it is." She stared at me, her dark brown eyes really intense thanks to the makeup. "So. Why are you here? Just for volunteer hours?"

"I need those, but this seemed like a good way to do it," I said. Did they have Heather grill all the volunteers? She was really good at it. I didn't think I could lie to her. Maybe it was the eyeliner? Intimidating.

"So you like dogs?" she said.

"I love dogs," I said. "But my dad's allergic, and a truck driver, and my mom works retail. Their schedules are random. We can't really have a dog, it wouldn't be fair with none of us home much." Repeating what my mom had said felt appropriate. Besides, it was true.

"Hm." Heather nodded once.

I felt like I just passed a test.

Instead of heading through the double doors where the barking was coming from, Heather led me in the other direction and we ended up in a small office with two desks. Filing cabinets filled one wall. On either side of the door, two big calendars on whiteboards were covered in multi-coloured notes. It looked complicated but organized.

I bet my mom would love the calendars.

"Okay," Heather said. "Have a seat." She pointed at the chair opposite the desk and sat. There was already a folder out, and she opened it.

I sat.

"This is the boring stuff," she said. "You have to read it and sign it and then I have to sign it. Mostly it says if anything awful or traumatic happens to you, Rescues in Motion won't get sued by your grieving family when we give them what's left of your body."

I stared at her. "For real?"

"No." She smirked. "Well, kind of. There's

a bunch of legal stuff that says we're not liable for accidents if you don't follow the rules, but everything is common sense." She shrugged. "We get funding — scraps — from the province. It means there are strict rules we have to follow."

"Right," I said, and started reading and signing. Heather wasn't kidding when she said it was boring, but I got through it. I was pretty sure I even understood most of it.

When I was done signing, Heather looked over everything, and she signed a few pages as well, then slid it back into the file and said, "Okay. Let's get it over with. *Parasites*!" She spread her fingers and widened her eyes, saying the word with drama.

"Okay." I tried not to laugh.

"Sometimes dogs we get from shelters or other programs are sick. They have parasites. Worms, mostly. When you do poop patrol, you're going to wear bags on your boots, gloves on your hands, and use a metal scooper for the poop." She lifted her hands. "That's pretty much the whole parasite speech — at least for what you'll be doing to start — but Jonas would freak if I didn't start there."

I did laugh now. It felt good.

"You're laughing," she said. "But a lot of volunteers don't realize they've signed up for a lot of dog poop." She stared me down until I stopped laughing, because was that *all* I'd be doing?

Finally, she cracked another smile. "You'll also maybe get to bottle-feed puppies if we end up with a mom who can't nurse, which is sort of the best thing ever. And enrichment and play time. But I really want you to prepare yourself for a lot of poop, okay? Trucks of poop. So. Much. Poop." She lifted both hands. "Picture waves of poo. Poo tsunamis. *Poo*-namis."

"Got it." I really liked Heather. "I don't mind." And surprisingly, I meant it. I mean, I wasn't looking forward to it or anything, but Heather seemed fun. Jonas wasn't too bad, even if he seemed permanently set to awkward-happy.

Forty hours with Heather or Jonas wouldn't be bad. And there'd be dogs.

I'd handle the poop.

"Let's take a tour," she said. "Then we can figure out when you can volunteer, and get you into the schedule. Was getting here at this time easy?"

"One bus right after school, yeah," I said.

"That's *great*," Heather said. "Most of our people can't get here until after five or six on weekdays. We'll show you how to do each thing as you do it. You'll get partnered with me or other senior volunteers until you've got it down. We tend to work in pairs."

She got up. I followed.

Behind the main building, Rescues in Motion's big fenced-off backyard broke into three different dirt-and-gravel yards with more fences and the double-gates I'd seen before. Heather said everyone called them "airlocks" just to annoy Jonas, who she said liked *Star Trek* way too much.

"He can't stop himself from telling us the fences aren't air-tight," Heather said. "It's incredible. You can see him *trying* to let it go, but he can't."

After my tour, Heather showed me how the metal

scoops worked for picking up poop. They were sort of like the things janitors used. I learned where the gloves and boot-bags were, and how to put them on and take them off, which was more difficult than I thought it would be. I took a few tries to get it right, and definitely appreciated learning how to take them off before I'd touched or stepped in anything.

The time flew by. Just as we were coming around the side of the building for me to grab my stuff and go home, a van pulled up.

"Ah! You'll see some chaos." Heather grinned. "One of our vans is back with a load of new dogs."

It didn't look like chaos. The van stopped on the far side of the gated driveway, and the driver door opened. A tall, lean, bearded man wearing a turban got out. He waved to Heather as he opened the driveway gate, backed the van through it, then got back out again to close the gate. When he went to the back of the van and opened the door, the passenger side door opened and another person climbed out.

A *familiar* person.

Oh no. Please no.

Unlike the first man, who I guessed was around forty, the second guy was my age. Scratch that, I knew he was one year older. Dark hair, tall, really great shoulders and *ridiculously* good-looking, he also waved at Heather before joining the guy at the back of the van and climbing in.

"You okay?" Heather asked. She stared at me, frowning in a way that reminded me of my mom. She even had a line between her eyebrows.

"Sure," I said.

I wasn't, though.

Because the other volunteer with the driver helping pull a big, black and white dog out of that van? I knew him. I knew what he looked like with his shirt off, thanks to a picture. And his name, from Mason's phone along with that picture.

Oliver.

That was Oliver.

Mason's Oliver.

04 Today's Gay Agenda: Doubt

HEATHER SAID SOMETHING about always moving the dogs one at a time but I didn't really hear it.

Oliver was here, helping the other volunteer get dogs out of the van. Oliver volunteered for Rescues in Motion. If Oliver volunteered here then . . .

Then what?

I stared as Oliver was handed a leash by the other volunteer, and a black dog jumped down and followed him down the narrow, fenced pathway behind the building. It seemed distracted and a little nervous. The dog kept putting his head low and its tail drooped between its legs. Oliver had to keep talking to it to get it to move forward, but they eventually got where they were going, using the large double-doors that led into the back of the building.

"Most of these dogs came from city shelters," Heather said. "They've already been checked and started meds. They mostly need somewhere to stay, which is always our biggest problem."

When Oliver returned, the man handed him another dog, brown and white and much smaller. Oliver carried it inside, not even putting it on the ground, though he still had it on a leash.

The doors closed behind him. I sighed. What was I going to do?

"You sure you're okay?" Heather said.

"Sorry." I turned back to her. I'd figure out how to react to Oliver later. Did it mean I'd need to quit? I hoped not. I didn't have another volunteer option lined up. But did I want to volunteer with Oliver?

No. No, I did not. This sucked.

Heather was still staring at me like she could tell I *wasn't* okay, so I asked a question. "Do all the dogs come from shelters?"

"Most," Heather said. "Or other rescue groups. We've got a bunch of vans and drivers and fosters, which is why we're Rescues in *Motion*. Finding places where dogs can get better if they're sick, get socialized, and eventually a permanent home." She shrugged. "It takes time. Most shelters don't have room for that kind of time." She sounded frustrated, but in a way she was used to.

I nodded. It made sense.

While we were talking, something seemed to get out of hand in the van. The other volunteer and Oliver had both climbed in, but instead of coming right back, there was this long, wailing-shouting noise, which made me jump because if it came from a dog, the dog sounded upset.

But when it stopped, I could hear Oliver and the other guy *laughing*.

Heather snorted. I looked at her. She seemed relaxed and shook her head, so whatever was happening wasn't a disaster.

Just loud.

"What's that?" I asked when another round of wailing came out from the van. It wasn't barking. More like rumbling grumbles and growling, only really, really loud.

"Probably our new husky," Heather said. "They tell it like it is."

"A husky?" I looked back at the van. I'd always thought huskies were gorgeous, like wolves. Seeing a husky might take the sting out of maybe having to quit Rescues in Motion on day one because my ex-boyfriend's boyfriend worked here.

Or volunteered. Whatever.

Before I could decide, though, both of the guys in the van laughed again — then one of them yelped — and a red-brown dog jumped out of the back of the van and bolted. I didn't know huskies could be that colour, but maybe this wasn't the husky? It was pretty big, though.

And *fast.*

"And we have a runner." Heather jogged toward the van. I ran after her, but it wasn't like the dog had anywhere it could go. They'd closed the driveway gate. The dog could run the length of the fenced corridor that led to the building and back to the van. Everywhere else had a gate.

Oliver and the other volunteer jumped down from the back of the van by the time we got there. The dog had run back and forth at least a half-dozen times already, and showed no signs of slowing down.

Oliver reached for the dog, and it dashed away again.

Smart dog, I thought.

"She might need zoomies," Heather said.

"You think?" the other volunteer said, laughing.

Heather opened the gate between the narrow corridor and the middle field where I'd trained on scooping up poop and hosing down the gravel. "Hey, pretty girl!" she said, raising her voice.

The dog stopped running, and *wow.*

The dog's eyes were the brightest blue I'd *ever* seen. I didn't get a very long look, though, because the dog saw the opening and launched herself, blasting past us both and running in big circles all around the edge of the yard. Her back claws kicked up gravel. I'd never seen a dog run like that before, landing on their front paws first, then their back paws.

"You two go ahead." Heather closed the gate. "We'll tire her out."

"She's skittish around men," Oliver said. He paused, looking at me and frowning, like he'd just noticed me, which was probably true.

"Oh," Oliver said.

Oh. That about summed it up.

I didn't throw up, so that was something. What I did do was sort of nod at him as casually as I could, then asked Heather, "What should we do?"

She looked at me, looked at Oliver, and then at me again.

"This way," she said, and I finally took a breath as we walked away from the van, and the volunteer, and freaking *Oliver.*

The dog was still running in circles, and she showed no signs of slowing down. Heather waited until we were away from the driveway then stared at me. I flinched.

"So," Heather said. "You know Oliver, I take it?"

Crap. I forced a smile. "Sort of. Not really. Kind of."

She narrowed her eyes. "And you . . . hate him? Or . . . ?"

I groaned. How could I explain? To even start I'd have to come out and . . . I shook my head and did my best to channel Nico. Nico always said coming out got easier each time. Also, my school put Rescues in Motion on their poster board. I didn't think they'd do that if the people who ran Rescues in Motion were homophobes. They'd had that thing about not allowing any form of discrimination on their website.

And the hot guy in the rainbow flag kilt kissing that dog.

Safe to say I could probably come out to Heather.

Only then I realized I couldn't. Or at least, I couldn't explain Oliver, not with any details. Because what if Oliver wasn't out to Heather?

I didn't want to out someone. Not even Oliver.

"I don't hate him." I didn't hate Oliver. Or, well, I didn't think I did. I mean, I didn't know him much. "He's friends with my ex." That was sort of the truth. Sure, Mason would object to "ex," and Oliver probably thought of himself with a different word than "friend," but whatever.

"Oh." Heather nodded. "You and your ex don't get along?"

I shook my head. I noticed the husky had finally stopped zooming around, and stood staring at us, panting, pink tongue out, and looking really, really proud of herself. Her bright blue eyes were *incredible*. Now that she'd stopped running, I could see white markings on her chest and legs, and patterns in her coat of lighter and darker shades of reddish-browns. "I've never seen a brown husky before."

"Brown is rarer," Heather said. I wondered if she

knew I wanted to change the subject. "She's definitely not purebred. If I remember the paperwork, she's from Manitoba, so probably she's a blend of northern dogs."

"Northern blend," I said. "Sounds like coffee."

Heather smiled. "Okay, that's a *great* name for her. Coffee. All that energy, and the brown fur?"

"She doesn't have a name?" How could such a pretty dog not already have a name?

"No owner. They found her wandering." Heather shook her head. "There'll be a temporary name in her file, but they suck at names. Trust me, yours is better."

I turned to look at the dog, which still stared at us warily. She hadn't come any closer, though she'd lowered her head to look up at us. Mostly she looked poised to sprint again. "What do you think?" I said. "You want to be called Coffee?"

She blinked. I reached out my hand. She lifted her head and took a single step further from me.

Ouch.

Well, Oliver said skittish, right?

"Here," Heather said, reaching into her pocket. I

held out my hand, and she handed me a little bone-shaped cookie. “First dog lesson. Crouch down and turn away from her, but hold your hand out where she can see it. Don’t make eye contact. Stay still, offer the treat. Let her come to you.”

I did what she said, crouching down first, then holding out the treat while looking off to the side. I could see her out of the corner of my eye.

Coffee’s head lowered, then raised. She took one step, then another. It took her a while to come all the way over, but when I felt the brush of her mouth on the flat of my palm, it took everything I had not to cheer. She nabbed the treat and took a few steps back to eat it, but when I rose, she didn’t run away. She watched me, though.

“It’s good she’s food-motivated. Not all huskies are. I’ll go get a leash,” Heather said. “Here. Keep going.” Heather handed me two more cookies.

Heather left. Coffee watched her go, but her bright blue eyes went right back to me the moment Heather left. Or to my hand.

She'd seen the cookies.

I crouched again, and did the same thing as before, letting her take the cookie without looking at her. She did, her mouth barely brushing my palm to grab the treat and taking a few steps away to eat it. I smiled at her, and she lowered her head again and let out a low, rumble-and-growl noise. It didn't sound anywhere near as frantic as before. If anything, it was more like Coffee was talking. And if I had to guess, she was telling me to *hurry the heck up already*.

"You want the last one?" I held up the cookie.

Another grumble. It almost sounded like "I want." I mean, not really, but Coffee's growly, rumbly voice was awesome.

She definitely wasn't shy about talking to me, even if she kept her distance.

Heather returned with a leash, so I did the crouch-and-turn thing again, and Coffee had crunched her way through the third treat by the time Heather got to us. Getting the leash on Coffee took effort — and two more cookies — but Heather finally got it on her, and we went to the kennels inside the building, where lots of dogs were waiting.

A few of them came up to the front of their individual stalls, tails wagging, but a lot of them stayed at the back, watching with wary, sad eyes.

When we got to the stall for Coffee, Oliver and the other volunteer were there, and Heather introduced me. The other volunteer was Harvinder, and he was another vet tech. I shook Harvinder's hand.

Oliver just stood there like he wasn't an asshole who messed around with other people's not-boyfriends.

"We're naming this one Coffee," Heather said, pointing at Coffee. The husky was currently scraping at the blanket over her dog bed in the corner of her stall in between circling over and over. "Beck's idea."

Harvinder laughed. Oliver said, "Nice name."

Okay. I guess we were doing polite, then?

"Thanks." I tried to sound the same.

Oliver and Harvinder went to go clean the transport cages, leaving Heather and me where we were.

I finally asked the question I'd wanted to know

since I'd seen Oliver climb out of the van.

"Does Oliver volunteer here often?"

"Quite a bit." Heather obviously knew what I was really asking, because then she said, "You'll probably work together."

"Well," I said, because that would suck, but it didn't have to be the end of the world, right? "We don't have to like each other to wear boots and gloves and pick up poop, right?"

"True." Heather tilted her head. "But it's more fun when you've got someone to talk to."

Beside us, Coffee finally lay down, heaving a massive sigh. I looked at her. Her bright blue eyes were aimed right at me, even though she had her nose buried under her fluffy tail. I swear she'd listened to every word I'd said.

And she looked doubtful.

I took a photo of her. A doubtful husky was perfect for Today's Gay Agenda.

05 Today's Gay Agenda: Ice Cream for One

"HOW WERE THE DOGS?" my mom asked, once I got my coat and shoes off. She sat at the kitchen table, with the family calendar and her to-do list journal.

"Adorable. But sad." I pulled out a chair and joined her. "There was a new dog today, and she was scared of us. I got to name her. Coffee. She's a husky, but she's brown and white. And she has blue eyes."

My mom smiled. "Sounds pretty."

"Here." I showed her the photo.

"Oh, she's *gorgeous.*" Mom gave me her serious look. "You do remember we can't have a dog, right?"

"I remember," I said, laughing. "Also, she's kind of afraid of men."

"You're right, that is sad." My mom looked at me, and I think she could tell I wasn't as happy as I was pretending to be. "Did you have a good time?"

"I did." I lifted my shoulder. Except for the Oliver part, but that was not something I intended to get into with my mom. I just couldn't. I could, however, talk about other parts of Rescues in Motion. "I learned how to pick up dog poop."

It made her laugh, like I'd hoped. "I wouldn't have thought that took much learning."

"They have scoops, and you have to wear gloves and put plastic boot-covers on, because of parasites." I raised one finger and tried to imitate Jonas's over-the-top voice. "We don't want parasites."

My mom grimaced. "Gross."

"Very."

"Are the people nice?" she said.

Everyone but Oliver. "I met Jonas and Harvinder. They're vet techs. Jonas was sort of awkward. Heather did the training stuff I did today. She's really cool. She taught me how to hold out a dog treat, and not look, so Coffee would be brave enough to come get it."

"The dog wouldn't even take a treat?" Mom put a hand over her heart. "Oh."

"She did eventually," I said. "Not making eye contact is the trick."

She shook her head like that wasn't much better. "Well, give me your schedule with them so I can add it to the family calendar. We can figure out meals and stuff."

"Okay," I said. "I'm being trained this weekend, both days, noon to three, and they'll give me my schedule after that — mostly right after school for an hour, not weekends. Today was paperwork and poop."

"You're going to talk about poop a lot, aren't you?" She narrowed her eyes but I could tell she found it funny.

"I'll try not to." We both knew I was lying. If I had to spend hours picking up dog poop, I'd share the misery.

"Uh-huh." Mom glanced at her notebook, then closed it. "Homework now, or do you want to help me with dinner? Grilled cheese and tomato soup."

"Dinner," I said, getting up. Grilled cheese was easy, and I didn't feel like diving into physics yet. "I don't have a lot, I can do homework after."

"Okay." We did our usual routine, working side-by-side, but she didn't have to tell me what to do. We'd had grilled cheese and tomato soup a lot when it was the two of us. Super-easy, and one of my mom's favourites. My dad didn't like it much.

"Speaking of tomorrow." My mom stirred the soup. "I'm closing the store. If Mason is coming over, either reheat something or make a stir-fry, okay?"

"Sure." I used my best "everything is totally fine" voice. I looked at her, smiled, and didn't twitch at Mason's name.

"What's wrong?" She frowned.

Ugh. This is why I was never going to be an actor. Also, I hate talking in front of crowds. Actually, I hate anything where people pay attention to me. I flipped the two sandwiches in the pan so I didn't have to look at her.

"Uh." Even without looking at her, I could feel my throat getting raw and I had to blink a bunch. I cleared my throat. "We broke up."

I finally looked at her. *Please don't ask questions.*

"Oh." Mom sort of went *still.* Her expression shifted somewhere between sad and something else — confusion, maybe? "I'm sorry." The way she said it, it almost sounded like a question.

It hit me what was happening. My mom had *no idea* how to comfort her son getting dumped by his boyfriend.

She's great, and always supportive, don't get me wrong. But the thing is, I think she'd always looked forward to my first girlfriend.

Okay, maybe that's putting it too strongly. More like she wanted to make sure I'd be a good boyfriend.

Ever since I was little she talked about how girls and women should be treated by boys and men, explaining stuff that makes life harder for women, and how that stuff hurts men too.

Then I came out, and she stopped talking about relationships.

She still points out sexism, toxic masculinity, all that stuff, but she doesn't aim it at me. It's not "when you're dating don't assume she'll do the cooking" anymore. Now, she points out how cooking and feeding a family is a full-time job, and most people just expect women to do it, and how boys don't often even get taught how to cook.

Which is wrong.

It's why I know grilled cheese, and stir-fries, and use the slow cooker, and all sorts of other recipes.

"Are you okay?" She stopped stirring the soup and put her hand on my shoulder.

Gah. Abort.

"Yeah," I said quickly. "I'm okay. It's okay." It wasn't okay, but it wasn't like she could do anything about it.

"Do you want to talk about it?" She looked so scared I'd say "yes" I nearly laughed, except it was only half funny and half I didn't know what, but made my throat hurt. The last time she'd looked like this was the second time she sat me down to talk sex.

Yeah, two sex talks.

The first time, she'd given me a really *detailed* talk about men and women having sex. She'd been totally cool and calm. Me, I'd spent the whole time with my stomach tying itself up in knots because all the stuff she was telling me was . . . Well.

Stuff I didn't want to do.

Then I came out, and talk number two.

Mom talking *gay* sex? *Awful.* So awkward, not at all cool or calm. She'd done her best. I mean, clearly, she'd read a lot of books, but I cannot tell you how embarrassing it is to hear your *mother* say the word "anal."

Telling Mom about Mason? That maybe he'd been seeing Oliver all along? Admitting I'd gotten everything wrong and Mason and I were never boyfriends in the first place? Oh, and bonus: Oliver volunteered at Rescues in Motion on a regular basis!

No. A world of no. Not going to happen.

"No." I shook my head. "It's okay."

"Well," she said. "Maybe have a friend over. Nico? A.J.? There's ice cream."

I almost laughed again. Did she think gay guys invited their friends over and cried into their ice cream after a breakup?

Actually, that sounded kind of awesome right now.

Only, if I asked Nico, would he even come over? A.J.? Any of the group from school? This was part of why I couldn't talk to Mom. She didn't get what it was like to be a queer guy. Or queer at all. I had *six* friends. That's it.

Or I used to.

Giving Mason space isn't a bad idea. Nico's text message. Nothing from the rest of them. Not even "how are you?"

"Soup is ready," my mom said.

"So are these." I used a spatula to put the first grilled cheese onto a plate.

***

After reading time was done, I grabbed my phone.

Nico's dog emojis were still there.

I still had no idea what to say. I sent him a smiley.

Grey dots popped up. I held my breath.

How was the dog place? He'd followed it up with two more dog emojis, and then a smiley.

Depends on how you feel about parasites and dog poop. I exhaled, relieved. Then added a few poop emojis for emphasis. **Dogs are great but sad. So many dogs with nowhere to go. How was Bruce House?**

Same? Mostly good, some sad. He added a rainbow flag, then kept going. **We got split into groups. Mostly we'll be packing food, answering phones, boring stuff.**

Split into groups. Maybe I should have gone with them after all. I might have been assigned to Nico's group, actually seeing and hanging out with him, instead of texting. I might not have seen Mason at all.

I started typing again — maybe I'd ask him over this weekend like Mom said — but his next message popped up before I could finish.

BUT! Free condoms and lube!

I laughed, and deleted what I'd written, starting over with, Well, that makes it all worthwhile, right?

Stocking up for a major slutty phase.

I laughed again. Someone in mind?

MULTIPLE hot cubs at BH.

I smiled. Nico liked stocky guys. I met a pretty lady named Coffee.

I'm sorry? Her NAME is Coffee?

Brown husky. I named her. I took a deep breath. And you'll never guess who dropped her off.

Who?

I hesitated. Maybe I shouldn't have said anything.

WHO?

Too late. I bit my lip. Oliver. I wrote, then realized Nico might need context — which sucked — and added, Mason's boyfriend. Then I erased *boyfriend* before I hit send, changing it to Mason's whatever.

I paused again. Too bitter? Too bitter.

BECK!!! Nico didn't do patience.

I changed it back to *boyfriend* and hit send.

Oh.

That's what Oliver said, too. Not helpful. "Oh" didn't really say anything.

Yeah. I wrote. Wasn't expecting it.

Mason introduced him to us. He seems nice.

I stared at my phone. Mason introduced Oliver to everyone. Nico thought he *seemed nice.*

I closed my eyes. My chest tightened and my eyes burned. This sucked so very much. Not only was Oliver at Rescues in Motion, Mason showed him off to our friends? God. I swallowed a couple of times. When I looked back at my phone, Nico hadn't said anything else.

Oliver seemed nice. Wasn't that the most perfect thing ever?

I sighed.

Catch you later, I wrote. Suddenly, the last thing in the world I wanted was Nico over on the weekend.

So much for crying into ice cream with my gay friends.

06 Today's Gay Agenda: Say No

USUALLY, FRIDAY ENDED with hanging out for a while in the GSA room, but now they were all heading to Bruce House, and I . . .

Wasn't.

Funny how you can have important things in your life one moment and then they're gone.

Same with friends.

When stuff goes wrong, Mom says "on the plus side" a lot. She says focusing on that helps. I wasn't feeling it. I headed straight to the bus, taking photos as I walked. Nothing really stuck. I didn't have a shot for Today's Gay Agenda yet. Some days are like that. I'd keep taking photos and hope something good came of it.

I lined up a shot of the bicycle rack.

An unknown number text popped up on my screen.

Any chance you're up for walking some dogs?

Probably Rescues in Motion, then.

My phone vibrated again.

This is Heather btw, not a parasite.

I smiled. No one at home waiting for me. It wouldn't matter if I went there instead. I eyed the clear sky. A bit chilly, but I had my jacket. I saw the bus I took to Rescues in Motion approaching, too.

That felt like a sign.

Sure, I texted back. Just leaving school, but I'm on my way.

After sitting, I added Heather to my contacts and managed to get my English class reading done. *The*

Great Gatsby continued to be boring, though I'd talk it over with my mom later. She explained school books and made them more interesting sometimes, but I will never understand the books we're forced to read.

Like, *The Great Gatsby*? Not one likeable character. Not a single character in the whole book I care about, except *maybe* Nick, the guy telling the story. Everyone is awful. Everyone is straight. Well, Ms. Lascos made a huge deal about Nick leaving a party with "a pale feminine" dude, with Nick the next day talking to the guy and the guy only wearing underwear.

Ms. Lascos was all, "*See*?"

Was I supposed to throw rainbow confetti? Even if it meant Nick Carraway was bi, it didn't come off as good.

Then again, I don't think anything in *The Great Gatsby* is supposed to be good. Mom says it's mostly how the "American Dream" is a lie. So, the whole point of the book is everything everyone thinks will be good for them, or will make them happy, doesn't?

Super depressing, really.

Also, this is Canada. Who cares about the American dream?

At least Cherie Dimaline's *Funeral Songs for Dying Girls* was next. Hopefully, something not written in the nineteen-hundreds will be a bit more relevant. After that, it's independent reading. I hadn't picked yet, but I wanted nothing told by a boring straight dude. Ms. Lascos really wanted us to read stories from new voices, so I absolutely wanted a queer book by a queer author.

I finished the chapter and got off the bus at Rescues in Motion in a pretty good mood. Heather sat behind the desk, and she seemed really happy to see me, which was kind of awesome.

"Thank you *so much*," she said. "We got six new dogs from a shelter in Hamilton and they've been in vans all day getting here. They need a walk." She blew out a sigh. "I'd promise we don't text begging for extra shifts, but we totally do. You can say no, though." She tilted her head and offered a wicked kind of smile. "Actually, that's generally a good life lesson."

"It's okay," I said. "My mom isn't home tonight so I'm on my own. This is more fun than homework."

"Just one hour," Heather said. "If you walk three dogs for twenty minutes each, between you and Oliver that'll do it? He'll show you."

I tried not to flinch at Oliver's name, or the way Heather had said it like a question. Was this one of those times I could say "no"?

Not likely.

Besides, pretty much the moment she said Oliver's name, in walked Oliver, like she'd summoned him. Heather did look like a witch, but it probably wasn't magic.

Just my life, sucking beyond the telling.

"Speak of the devil," Heather said to Oliver, then glanced at me, and I realized she was still waiting for me.

I nodded.

Heather smiled. "Great."

Oliver sort of *paused*. He eyed Heather, then me, then said, "Hi."

“Hi,” I said.

Yeah, this would be awful.

“Six new dogs.” Heather sounded like the cheerleaders when our basketball team was having an off game and they tried to make up for it being perky. “If the two of you take one each, ten minutes out, ten minutes back, we can have them all walked before dinner. Oliver, you know the routine — show Beck?” Heather spoke to Oliver like he was in charge.

My gut sank. He totally was. Super.

“Sure thing.” Oliver faced me with this really *polite* look on his face. “This way.” He gestured to the two big doors.

This was going to suck.

Chopper, the big yellow dog I leashed first, wanted to choke himself. He pulled from one tree to the next, yanking with all the strength he had, making himself cough and gasp because he pulled the collar against his throat so tight.

"Woah," I said, trying to tug him back a bit.

It made him pull harder.

Beside me, Oliver had the opposite problem. The smallish brown Buckley stopped to sniff the light pole right outside Rescues in Motion and didn't seem to care to ever move on.

"Buckley," Oliver said, in a patient, sing-song voice. "Hey, pup."

Buckley kept sniffing the pole.

We had treats and poop bags and gloves, but since these dogs had come from a Hamilton shelter, they'd already had their shots and medical once-over.

No doubt Chopper was healthy. The dog was *strong*. I tried not to get too far ahead of Oliver, but totally lost that battle. Chopper wanted to get to the next thing. As soon as possible.

At least Oliver got Buckley away from the first lamp pole.

Then again, if I got far enough ahead we could spend the next hour without speaking. That would be nice.

"So we usually head toward the park." Oliver pointed. "Loop around the outside of the park, down the side streets until we hit ten minutes. Then turn around and come back."

"Right," I said.

Chopper lunged at a squirrel, yanking me hard. Luckily, the squirrel scrambled up a tree before I fell down. Chopper stopped, stared straight up the tree, and whined.

"You okay?" Oliver sounded like he was trying not to laugh.

"Yeah," I said.

Chopper's big brown eyes turned to me, like I could fix it.

"Dude, I can't make it come back," I said. At least he wasn't pulling.

Chopper whined again. I scratched between his ears. The moment I touched his head, Chopper threw himself down on the ground and rolled onto his back, legs splayed and tongue hanging out.

"I think he wants belly rubs," Oliver said.

You think? I bit back snapping at Oliver and gave Chopper belly rubs. It didn't last. Four seconds later he'd had enough, jumped back on his feet, and pulled.

"If you use the second loop on the leash it'll be easier to control him." Oliver said it in that polite way again, like he was giving a report at the front of a class. "It's good at lights, intersections, anywhere you need to keep the dog close. Like this."

The Rescues in Motion leashes had two handles, a second loop about halfway down the length of the leash. I slipped my left hand into it the same way Oliver held his, gripping the other end of the leash with my right hand.

Oliver was right. Much easier. Chopper pulled, but he couldn't zig-zag.

"He's got labrador retriever in him," Oliver said, coming up alongside me now that Chopper wasn't swinging like a wrecking ball. Buckley trotted beside him like a perfectly happy and well-trained dog.

So annoying.

Chopper pulled, coughing again. Still, we were

moving forward, which was all we needed to be doing to make this end sooner.

"His head shape isn't lab, though. Chopper might have great dane in him, too," Oliver said, after another few moments of quiet. "But this little guy is all beagle."

Great. Dog facts. Would Oliver be all chatty the entire next hour of our lives? I glanced at him while he looked at Buckley and thought about what Heather said about saying no being a life lesson.

Maybe this was one of those times?

"I don't really want to talk," I said. Oliver's brown eyes widened like he was surprised.

"Oh." He sounded offended. "Okay," he said, in a way that said it wasn't okay at all. Probably tall, cute, polite Oliver didn't meet many people who didn't want to talk to him.

It honestly pissed me off a little. I sighed, annoyed.

"Dude, fine." He lifted up a hand.

"You already got Mason, okay?" As soon as the words were out, I wished I could take them back. Too late.

Oliver blinked. "What?"

"Look." I took a deep breath, not wanting to sound pathetic. "I don't really want to talk with the guy my ex-boyfriend replaced me with." *Shit.* No. Mason had *never* been my boyfriend. "Sorry. That's not . . ." I shook my head. I did *not* want to apologize to Oliver. I *wasn't* sorry. "Never mind. Let's just walk dogs," I said. "Tell me what to do, I guess, but . . . just dogs. Okay?"

So much for not sounding pathetic. Chopper tugged, but Oliver didn't move.

He just frowned at me. In fact, he stared until it got uncomfortable.

"What?" I definitely didn't sound friendly. Chopper glanced back at me, and I gestured to the big yellow dog. "We need to keep going."

"Right." Oliver shook his head, but he didn't say anything else. He led Buckley forward.

Chopper wasn't the only one happy to get moving. *Finally.*

We looped around the park in silence, and by

the time we were heading back, Chopper wasn't choking himself as often. We swapped for two new dogs — Marty and Rosie — did the entire walk again in complete silence, and then took the final two new dogs for their walk.

My last dog, Cinnamon, was jumpy and sad, reminding me a bit of Coffee, though Cinnamon wasn't a husky. Patches of Cinnamon's curly reddish-brown fur had been shaved, and she cowered when a bus passed.

"Try giving her a cookie when you see buses or trucks coming." Oliver broke the silence. "Take her aside, have her focus on you. It'll teach her not to be afraid of the noise."

Oliver sounded like he knew his stuff. I tried it when I spotted a truck coming.

I petted Cinnamon before the truck passed, and fed her a treat. She still cowered, but seemed less upset than before. Once we were walking again, I caught Oliver giving her sad looks in between dealing with his little chihuahua, Chico. Chico walked fearlessly, and wanted to catch squirrels even more than Chopper.

When we returned them to their kennels, I caught Oliver staring again. As much as I wanted to stare back — I did *not* want to be the pathetic loser ex — I couldn't handle his dark brown eyes.

He'd looked at Cinnamon the same way. Pitying.

Heather closed up the kennels. Every spot was full. I kept my attention on the dogs, but Oliver stood right beside us. Hard to ignore.

After Heather locked up Chico and Cinnamon, she eyed me. "Want to say hello to Coffee before you go?"

It felt like her giving me an out. I took it.

"Sure," I said.

Oliver drifted away in the other direction though I swear I felt him staring at the back of my head. Heather and I found Coffee in her kennel. She looked up at us when we came into view, and tilted her head. She had her soft-looking bed in the corner of the kennel, her water and food bowl, and a rope toy, but her bright blue eyes still seemed afraid.

Heather unlocked her kennel and I stepped in. I decided not to face her directly, and crouched down with the last of my treat supply on my palm.

"Hey, Coffee," I said. "How you doing?"

It took her a second to take the cookies, but she did. There wasn't a lot of space in the kennel, so I stayed still. When I finally looked at her, she lowered her head, but didn't dash away.

I thought about trying to stroke her head, but remembered Heather's advice about going slow. "You have very pretty eyes."

Coffee's short grumble-growl *a-woo* sounded an awful lot like "I know."

"Thanks for coming in," Heather said. "We appreciate it. I'll try not to ask too often."

"It's fine." I rose. Coffee watched me intently, but didn't move back, which made me feel kind of awesome. Once I was outside her kennel, she went back to her bed and circled a few times before lying down again and issuing the biggest sigh ever.

"So much drama." It reminded me of Nico.

"Huskies live for drama," Heather said. "She's getting more vocal. It's a good sign."

Good for you, Coffee. I smiled down at the red-brown husky, and she didn't look away. After a moment, she blinked a few times, then closed her eyes. Time for a nap, I guess.

I wasn't looking forward to going home, but I couldn't stay here.

"See you," I said to Heather, and headed out. I braced for Oliver, but didn't bump into him, and made it all the way to the bus stop without any drama of my own.

07 Today's Gay Agenda: Take Shots

BY MONDAY, I'd picked up poop, learned the hand signals Rescues in Motion used when training dogs, picked up more poop, walked nine different dogs over the weekend, picked up even more poop, and got to go with Heather in one of the vans to deliver Chico to a temporary home. It was with a retired librarian who'd taken half a dozen small dogs in the last two years until they found permanent homes.

"The people who give our dogs temporary

placement are amazing," Heather said. "We'd never manage to do what we do without them."

Heather's mood wasn't shared by Chico. The chihuahua basically *screamed* the entire ride. Heather said some dogs were like that. Car rides freaked them out.

I didn't bump into Oliver at my training shifts, and by the time I was halfway through my Monday at school, I figured Rescues in Motion would be good after all. I grabbed my lunch from my locker, deciding whether or not to eat outside. When I closed my locker door, Mason was standing right there.

Worst magic trick ever.

"Mason," I said. I wished I hadn't. I mean, he knew his own name. Way to state the obvious, Beck.

"What did you say to Oliver?" Mason's jaw was clenching. His grey eyes were snapping back and forth while he looked at me.

Was he *pissed*?

I froze. Avoiding Mason had been number one on my to-do list since the not-actually-a-break-up. I thought Mason felt the same way.

It took a second for his question to sink in. *What did you say to Oliver*?

"What?" Not a brilliant response, but I had no idea what he meant. Also, were people staring? It felt like people were staring. I looked around, but I didn't see Maya or any of the GSA group around.

He'd come alone?

And Mason had almost whispered.

Weird.

Normally Mason was louder than this, and he *always* had the group with him.

"What did you say to Oliver?" Mason repeated his question. "Did you lie to him about being my boyfriend? Because that's a dick move. I don't know why I have to keep saying this, but we were never boyfriends, Beck."

"Wait. No." I cringed. Because I *had* said that, yeah, but not like Mason made it sound. "I didn't *lie* —"

"Yes, you did." Mason cut me off. "Oliver said you called me your boyfriend."

"Because I *thought* —" I tried to calm down.

"No, you assumed." Mason shook his head. "Beck, we had fun. We hung out. But we were *never* boyfriends. Got it?" His voice rose, and even though the hallways were mostly empty for lunch, a couple of girls had noticed us. I was pretty sure they were grade nine kids, but still. "You need to get over your crush or whatever, because it's *not going to happen.*"

He held up both hands, doing a "keep away" thing, like I'd been the one to come bother him, and now he wanted me to leave.

"But you . . ." I started.

"I'm with Oliver," Mason said. "I'm sorry you're jealous. But you need to stop obsessing over me, okay? Just . . . *move on.* Leave me — and Oliver — alone."

He turned and walked away. I watched him go. Pretty sure my mouth hung open.

Did that really just happen?

One of the grade nine kids snickered. I was *done.* I gripped my lunch and turned around and headed in the opposite direction from Mason and the two girls.

I absolutely refused to melt down here. I wouldn't cry where *anyone* could see me, let alone two complete strangers who thought this was funny. I headed outside, looked for a spot where no one else was eating, and ended up sitting on the ground, leaning against the side of the school, and staring into space.

I didn't end up crying.

You need to get over your crush.

How was this my life? I patted my pockets, but my phone was still in my locker, and the thought of going back to grab it when I'd just have to put it away again before class seemed like too much effort.

Besides, who would I text?

I wondered where Mason was now. Usually, our group ate in the cafeteria, on the second table by the windows. Had he gone to tell them about his ambush at my locker?

Did they believe him about me lying to Oliver?

Was he *right*?

I closed my eyes.

Was Mason right? I couldn't shake the thought.

We'd never said we were dating, had we? Had I never called him my boyfriend in front of him? I swore I must have, but . . . It had only been a couple of weeks. Not even half of August. And we'd mostly been alone.

I couldn't *actually* remember.

He'd never used the word "love," and I hadn't had the courage. Mason always said "adore." When we were alone, he kissed my forehead when I said something fun or silly, and always said, "I adore you."

So I started saying it, too.

But now, remembering? He never said it in front of anyone else. He said he was nervous about being in public, which I totally understood. PDAs were scary. What if someone freaked out? But alone he wasn't shy. And he'd made the first moves there, right?

Yes.

All of them?

I mean, I thought so. I did not do first moves with guys as cute as Mason. The first time we'd gotten naked together, Mason had *definitely* been the one who'd started things. And after . . .

Same thing as always. He kissed my forehead.

I adore you.

Adore didn't mean he loved me or was my boyfriend, though, right? I'd never asked him out, not officially. We'd hung out a lot in August, then made out, then had sex . . .

Never saying *boyfriends*. Mason definitely felt clear about that. I'd just thought we were.

Then that photo and text from Oliver. Hot, shirtless Oliver, smiling at the camera and telling Mason he was home. Alone.

Ugh.

I opened my eyes and pulled out my apple. I took a bite, barely hungry.

What was I supposed to do? Nico said to give Mason space. I'd not heard from anyone else. They all hung out together, so I couldn't go ask for advice.

It wasn't like I could talk to my mom.

I mean, imagine it: "Hey, Mom, even though you always tell me how important consent and communication are, I totally fucked up and had sex with Mason without even finding out if he likes me, because I assumed he did."

That would not go well.

I mean, she'd give me bonus points for condom use, I suppose.

I groaned out loud.

If only Dad was home. No less embarrassing to tell Dad I was having ex-boyfriend drama — scratch that, not-even-an-ex-boyfriend drama — but he always listened.

I didn't know when his next rest day was, though. He basically drove his truck until he hit the limit of legal hours he could in a set number of days, then parked wherever he happened to be and slept for a day. That's when he'd call.

Long-distance trucker life.

I halfheartedly ate most of my lunch, and went back to my locker, keeping my head down but looking for Mason before every corner. I didn't see him, or anyone from the GSA. I put what was left of my lunch away and pulled out my phone. I had five minutes before class, but as I scrolled my texts, I couldn't bring myself to actually text someone.

Except . . .

Heather's text was there, the one where she'd asked me if I could walk dogs.

Why not? I tapped out a message.

Can I drop by when I'm not on the schedule? I looked at it for a second, trying to decide if it was pathetic, but the bell rang and I hit send. I grabbed my books and headed to class.

When the day was done, she'd answered.

It won't count for volunteer hours, but you're always welcome to give the dogs playtime or walks.

I shoved my homework into my bag and, for the first time since lunch, it didn't feel like a giant weight was crushing my chest from the inside-out.

I texted her back. **On my way.**

★★★

"Thanks for this." I threw the ball for Oscar the Wonder Schnauzer, who tore after it, but then sat down to give it a good chomp. Oscar loved chasing balls. Bringing them back? Not so much.

"The dogs are always up for more playtime," Heather said.

"Oscar sure is," I said.

Oscar rolled onto his back in the grass, chomping the ball in his mouth, holding it in place with his little front paws. I pulled out my phone, and snapped pictures while I lined up a good shot.

I'd learned that lesson the hard way: take shots while you aim. Sometimes, by the time you get everything where you want it? Too late. Something moves or changes.

Turned out that's double with dogs.

But Oscar seemed content to be his goofy self. I got a great shot of him, in good light, and a completely adorable pose. I grinned, showing Heather. "Want it for the website?"

I'd been too timid to ask before, but Oscar looked *awesome* in my photo.

"Yes!" Heather said.

"Okay," I said. "I love his write-up, but his photo makes him look boring, and he's *not* boring."

"I did the write-up." Heather sounded distracted and took my phone from me. "This is *really* good. Like, you can see he's awesome, but also *a lot*. Jonas takes the photos — he snaps them when they first get put in the kennels."

"Ah." This seemed like one of those moments where if you didn't have anything nice to say you shouldn't say anything.

Heather laughed and gave me my phone back. "Send it to me. I'll swap it." She pushed her hair behind her ear.

"Can I do more?" I asked.

"More photos of Oscar?"

"No, the other dogs," I said. "When I'm walking them or giving them playtime? Pictures that show off what they're actually like, I mean. I've already got some of Coffee." I gave Oscar a little rub on his head, then scrolled through my phone, finding one of the shots of Coffee I'd gotten where she was looking at me with attitude.

"Oh, wow. Yeah, send me that one, too," Heather said. "Does this mean you're not leaving?"

Wait. What? Leaving? "Sorry?" I blinked.

"When you asked to come by, I thought maybe something went wrong with Oliver and you were gonna bail." She tugged the ball free, which set Oscar off bouncing and barking. She threw it. Oscar zipped off to get it. "You really didn't seem to like Oliver, but that's not it, is it?"

Oscar sat where the ball was, chewing it. We walked over to him again.

"No," I said. "No, it's not him. Not exactly. He's . . . okay."

Honestly, Oliver kept being polite. Nice. I almost wished he'd be a jerk.

"But?" She raised one eyebrow and crossed her arms. Man, she was intimidating.

"Honestly, what's bugging me is it's all my fault," I said. "I screwed up, sort of, with my ex. But my ex and I have the same friends, and now my ex —"

"You can call him by his name," Heather said. "You don't have to avoid pronouns for me. We're good."

I laughed. "That obvious?"

"My gaydar is pretty solid. Unless it's a hot butch woman, in which case it fritzes, which is *really* annoying." She lifted one shoulder, but she smiled. "But at least with hot butch women, there's a good chance, right?"

"I'd say so." God, I liked Heather.

She pointed at me, rolling her finger in a "hurry-up" way.

Right. "Okay, so, my boyfriend and I broke up." I groaned. I'd done it again. *Boyfriend.* "Except no we didn't, because I assumed we were dating in the first place."

"Assumed?" Heather frowned.

"He never asked me out." Ugh. Every time I said it, it sounded worse. How could I have been so dumb? "I never asked him out, either, but we were, uh . . ." I wasn't sure how to explain.

"Hanging out?" Heather said. "Like, dates? Doing stuff together all the time?"

"Yeah," I said. "And, um." Okay, was I blushing? Pretty sure I was blushing.

"Sex." Heather nodded again. She wrestled the ball free for another throw. Oscar took off like a shot. "Got it."

"Right." I cleared my throat. Nico says I shouldn't be embarrassed talking about sex, but I don't think I'll ever get there. "Anyway, he's seeing someone else —"

"Oliver," Heather said. "He's seeing Oliver."

"Uh." I wasn't sure what to do here. Was Oliver out to Heather? It seemed likely, but I didn't know.

We walked to Oscar.

"It's okay, Beck," Heather said. "Oliver mentioned his name. Mason, right?"

I sighed. Yep. Oliver was out to Heather. I could stop twisting myself up worrying I'd accidentally out him. "Yeah." This time, Oscar let the ball go for me without too much effort, though as always he immediately started bouncing and barking.

"Dude, you gotta learn patience," I said to him. "Sit." I did the little turn of my wrist hand signal they used at Rescues in Motion.

Oscar technically sat. For, like, a second. Then he barked and ran in a little circle on the spot, like his energy had to go *somewhere* or he'd explode.

I threw the ball. He chased after it with joyful barks.

"So, Mason called it off?" Heather said.

"I saw a text I shouldn't have," I said, which again sounded worse out loud. "Only, since we weren't *actually* dating, I guess not?" I lifted one shoulder. I knew I sounded pathetic. "I got upset, and Mason said if I couldn't handle it, then maybe we should stop *hooking up*."

Upset was understating, but I didn't have to tell Heather I'd been gutted. What had Mason said today? I needed to *get over my crush*?

"So, you thought you were with him." Heather held up a finger while we walked. "He didn't tell you about other guys, but was seeing Oliver." She held up another finger. "You found out, and he broke off your thing." Her third finger went up. "Is that right?"

"That's right," I said, turning all my attention on Oscar. I couldn't bring myself to look Heather in the eye.

I also couldn't get Oscar to give me the ball.

"Okay, so, here's the thing," Heather said quietly. I turned to face her, wondering how much this would hurt. I imagined Heather didn't do gentle advice. Like, should I brace for impact? "I only have your side of it, obviously," she said, "but Mason sounds like a gaslighting asshole."

I opened my mouth.

I couldn't think of a single thing to say.

I closed my mouth.

"What?"

"I'm not saying you didn't make assumptions," Heather said, setting off another round of barking from Oscar by tugging the ball free and making him sit before she threw it again. "But you were definitely together. Sounds like he's using a technicality to say he didn't cheat." She tilted her head to one side. "He put it all on you. But if he'd never intended a relationship, it's at least *half* on him to say so." She crossed her arms. "He doesn't have to be monogamous, no one does, but everyone he's with should know that first. Only telling you *after* sleeping with you? Gaslighter move." She shrugged. "Trust me. I've had experience with people telling me everything is my fault for not reading their minds."

"Oh." I took a breath.

Huh.

08 Today's Gay Agenda: Crop the Shot

AFTER WE PUT OSCAR BACK, Heather needed to do some stuff in the office, and I decided to try taking Coffee for a walk. She let me leash her, which was progress, but when we got outside, she pulled toward the back fence airlock until she was at the very end of her leash.

Then she planted her feet and wouldn't move.

Turns out dogs can turn into boulders. I tried

treats, I tried asking her to follow me. I even tried sitting down and being smaller than her.

Nothing. She just kept staring at the fence.

I gave in.

"You just want to run in there?"

I swear Coffee understood me. Her whole body language changed, and she did a little jump as soon as I started moving toward her.

Once we were through the two fences and I undid her leash, she ran in big, looping circles, paws sending clumps into the air.

Zoomies, Heather called it. Coffee definitely zoomed.

I got shots of her in motion on my phone, and decided to practice getting her to come back. Rescues in Motion had two commands for this: *come*, where you put your fist against the centre of your chest and the dog was supposed to sit down in front of you, and *touch*, where you held your hand out to one side for the dog to bump with its nose.

Harvinder and Jonas wanted *touch* to be food

rewarded, always. As soon as the dog touched your palm, they got a treat. Every single time. No exceptions.

Touch was supposed to be the emergency command, working no matter what, so it got rewarded no matter what.

Coffee hadn't picked up on either yet. She did sometimes with Heather and some of the other women, but with me and any other guy? Not so much.

I ended up crouching and turning my hand out like always, keeping my head turned. I said "Touch" when she took a cookie.

That was how Heather said I could get Coffee to understand *touch* meant physically touching my hand for food.

Coffee's beautiful blue eyes stayed on me while she ate, but she wasn't crouching or flinching away from me the way she used to. She didn't run away from me.

At least, not until I tried to put her leash back on to bring her back inside. Then she became zoom-dog again.

Repeatedly. In fact, each time she seemed happier about it, tail wagging and ears going up and a big doggy smile, like this was the best game ever.

The fourth time I tried to leash her and she bounce-jumped away from me, I heard laughter, and realized I wasn't alone anymore.

Oliver was watching me. I guess he had a volunteer shift.

Super.

"Need help?" he asked.

I didn't want it, but I needed it.

"If you think you can," I said.

He came through the airlock. The moment he opened the first gate, Coffee lowered her head, watching him carefully. I could see her working out what to expect. She growly-grumbled at him, and her tail did the tiniest wag.

I think it translated roughly to "I'm not done, and you can't make me."

Oliver held out a treat, and said, "Touch."

Coffee growl-grumbled again. It seriously sounded

like "go away."

I laughed. Okay, maybe I enjoyed Coffee giving Oliver attitude.

"Not going to be fooled that easy, huh?" Oliver said.

More growly-grumbles, like she agreed with him. Coffee really was awesome when she talked. I lifted my phone and got a few shots.

She circled. Oliver crouched, treat out. She ran up and nabbed it and jumped back to crunch it happily. He held out another. And another.

Eventually, when she came for cookie number four, Oliver managed to hook his hand into her collar with a really quick flip of his wrist.

I didn't *want* to be impressed, but I was.

He caught me looking.

"Lots of practice," Oliver said. He attached the leash and stood up.

"Right." Did he have to be so gentle with the dogs, and so good at everything?

And so cute?

"I didn't think you were on the schedule today," Oliver said, the way you'd say, *I didn't see the dog shit I just stepped in.*

Oof.

"I wasn't," I said. "I should get home for dinner. I'll take her back inside."

"No, it's fine," Oliver said. "I'll walk her now you got her zoomies out."

"Okay." I headed for the airlock. He did the same. Not the most awkward thing ever, but close.

I headed for the bus stop, realizing that Oliver would *also* be walking that way. We'd be side-by-side until we got there. At least he'd keep going. It seemed to take forever to get there.

He didn't spout dog facts this time.

I unzipped my bag for my earbuds once I got there. Oliver stopped, so I just sort of stood there, holding them, feeling dumb.

"So," Oliver said. "Um . . ."

Please no. Was he going to talk to me about something that *wasn't* dogs? I mean, the only other topic we could possibly discuss was Mason and no. A world of no.

"It's fine." I blurted the words out. "Really."

Oliver frowned at me. He didn't look fine. I mean, he looked *cute*-fine, but not *okay*-fine.

I put my earbuds in. Not polite, but it worked.

Oliver left. Coffee turned back to look at me a couple of times, but Oliver didn't.

Thank God.

I played music, I texted my mom to let her know I'd gone to Rescues in Motion first, then scrolled photos, hunting for Today's Gay Agenda. I smiled at the shots of Coffee running like mad, and Oscar with and without the ball.

When I scrolled further back, Mason appeared.

August.

A lot of my Mason photos were basically selfies, our heads together, smiling up at the camera when we were alone. I'd also taken pictures of just Mason. I had a few of him reading after dinner on the other side of the couch from me — Mom would not be happy to know I snuck my phone into reading hour — and I stopped on one. Mason reading my favourite graphic novel, *You Brought Me the Ocean*, with this small smile. It looked like he'd just read something funny, but didn't want it to show.

He looked good. I mean, Mason always looked good. That photo? *Hello.*

That night, he'd slept over. Not that we spent much time sleeping.

Which meant Mom had been at work and I hadn't snuck my phone at all, come to think of it. I remembered. Mason teased me when I grabbed a book after dinner.

"Are we really going to do the reading thing even though your mom isn't here to make us?" he'd asked, laughing.

"Pick a book." I'd been trying to be funny, or cool, or *something*. Flirty, I guess? We both knew what would happen after, but me handing him a book and making him read for an hour first was . . .

Was what? Sexy? I don't know. Given how it

turned out, probably I wasn't any judge of sexy.

I closed the photo and kept scrolling.

In between shots for Today's Gay Agenda, Mason's face appeared again and again. A brick wall with a hand-painted smiley face that said "You are Beautiful!" beneath it. Mason in the sun, eyes closed, looking up. Pansies growing in a crack in the sidewalk. Mason smiling at me. And on and on . . .

Once I scrolled back further than August, pictures of Nico, Maya and Amélie, or A.J. started to appear, but even then? Mason. I'd had a crush on him for most of grade eleven, if I was being honest. This summer was the first time we'd hung out alone. Mason's face stuck out in any group photo I'd taken, usually right in the middle.

I stopped scrolling.

When I first started taking photos, I put whatever I was taking a picture of right in the middle. I didn't know much yet. I figured that's what you did. It wasn't until I read about composition that I found out putting the big thing right in the front and centre wasn't necessary.

In fact, framing things right in the middle of a photo *wasn't* a good idea.

Turns out photographs get more interesting to look at when you don't. One video I watched called it "the rule of thirds" but I picture a tic-tac-toe board — two vertical lines, two horizontal lines, breaking up a photo into nine equal rectangles. Any picture is more *interesting* if the important thing is at one of the four places where the lines cross, or if you line up some natural edge along one of the lines.

Like, if you put the horizon through the middle of a picture, it won't look as good as when the horizon is a third of the way from the bottom or the top. A statue or a person? Looks better when they stand a third of the way to one side.

Even the "you're beautiful!" smiley graffiti I found? I put it in the bottom right, where those two imaginary tic-tac-toe lines cross.

It's easy to follow the rule of thirds when cropping photos, but you need to think about it when you're taking photos, too. If you don't, you can forget you need extra room.

If you don't have room around the edges, you've got nothing you can crop. The thing you were taking a picture of stays in the centre, and it doesn't fit in a way that looks better.

You need space around something if you want to frame it right. It can't take up the whole view.

One thing shouldn't be the whole shot.

I moved my thumb on the screen, scrolling back and back until I found pictures that weren't Mason.

A.J. and I playing one of their endless board games. Maya and Amélie with their foreheads pressed together, adorable as hell, sitting on a fountain, downtown. Random shots of maple trees from last fall, when the leaves were changing from yellow to orange and red . . .

When I scrolled back down toward now, Mason came back, and everything and everyone else just sort of vanished. Even my Today's Gay Agenda photos were sometimes one-offs, where I'd thrown something together at the last minute because the day was almost done, and I'd been with Mason all day.

Maybe the rule of thirds applied to more than taking photos.

I'd put Mason right in the middle of my life, and I hadn't given myself enough room for anything else.

Maybe Heather was right, though. Mason put himself there, too. Had he done it on purpose? Let me think I'd done it all myself?

Either way, I felt like trying to crop my entire life but not having room left over to make a good picture.

So now what?

I scrolled to the latest photos I'd taken today. In the very last shot, Coffee was only half in the frame, and blurry. I shook my head. Coffee didn't make it easy. She'd sit, looking directly at me with those amazing blue eyes, and the moment I lifted my phone, she became a moving target again.

In fact, taking pictures for Rescues in Motion led to tons of blurry dog shots I couldn't use.

That reminded me of another video I'd watched

about taking photos. Bad shots were just a part of photography. One of the reasons I took a lot of photos, in fact.

I deleted the blurry Coffee photo, and scrolled back. There'd be one in the bunch I could use, or there wouldn't.

If there wasn't, I'd take more.

The bus appeared. I put my phone away long enough to tap my card and find a seat before I kept looking for a good shot.

I found one.

Coffee was running toward me, and her mouth was open, her ears were up, and her bright blue eyes focused right ahead. You saw how fast she was but you also saw how pretty she was, and the doggy joy on her face.

The only downside to the beautiful photograph being a *very* visible pile of dog poop in the background.

I fiddled with cropping, and found the sweet spot, framing her face in the top left with her feet at the bottom left. Twiddling the contrast made the lighter markings on her chest and legs and the underside of her curly tail draw your eyes around the photo.

The longer I looked, the more I found new things to like about Coffee.

Most importantly? No poop. Cropped right off the side.

Once I was sure I had it right, I sent it to Heather, then put my phone away, but I couldn't stop thinking about all those pictures of Mason.

I'd fucked up. In fact, I was pretty sure I'd fucked up pretty big, all things considered. Those photos, all of August, how *everything* had become all about Mason? My other friends vanishing?

Well.

Definitely time to crop some shit out.

09 Today's Gay Agenda: Be Patient

SHOCKINGLY, between school and Rescues in Motion, it turned out I preferred picking up poop.

I mean, not really, but dodging Mason sucked. He glared at me any time he spotted me. Given how fast Amélie left Physics class and how Maya was there waiting to lead her away, Maya and Amélie were definitely avoiding me, too.

I so didn't love school right now.

I spotted Nico a few times, but he was always with

at least part of the group — always including Mason — but I needed to start somewhere. With someone. So, Nico.

On the bus ride to Rescues in Motion on Friday after school, I sent Nico a shot of Coffee, and wrote: RIM bestie.

Nico reacted with a heart, and then the little grey dots bounced.

Your acronym is way funnier than mine, came his reply. RIM › whatever BH might be. This he followed with the peach and the smiley with its tongue sticking out. Rimming for everyone!

I burst out laughing, and typed: Pervert.

If you think rimming is perverted you've been gone too long.

Wasn't that just the truth. I sighed, glancing up to make sure I didn't miss my stop, trying to think of something to say. Any luck with the hottie at Bruce House? My thumb hovered. I hit send before I could change my mind.

Not yet. Cross your fingers.

Nico sent a photo next. Unsurprisingly, given Nico's tastes, a stocky, burly-looking dude, maybe a few years older than us with short, neat locs, warm brown skin, and one heck of a sly smile grinned right at the camera.

Okay, yes, cute. And he knows it. I hit send.

His name is Devon. RIM bestie-to-be. Or just rimming. I'm easy.

I laughed again. God, I missed Nico. The three grey dots bounced, so I waited.

But not cheap! This he followed up with multiple dollar signs.

My stop was coming up. I bit my lip, not sure if it was a good idea, but I really did miss Nico. Time to do something about it.

Meet for lunch tomorrow? I typed it in, then decided to be blunt. Hang out, just us?

The grey dots came and went twice. Can we do Friday?

Sure, I sent. Maybe the GSA was doing something tomorrow. And the day after.

Solo lunch for me in the field until Friday. Hooray.

I waited to see if he'd send more, but he didn't, and it was my stop. By the time I opened the door to Rescues in Motion, everything felt a bit more possible again. Jonas was talking with Harvinder at the front desk. I waved.

"Hey," I said. "How are the parasites?"

Harvinder laughed, but Jonas said, "The battles continue in our favour, but the war is far from won."

I blinked. He sounded serious. "Great."

"Oliver is already here. Scooping, then walks," Harvinder said. He smiled at me. "We haven't had a second to scoop today, but we saved Coffee for walks with you. Even though she yelled at me when I took Buckley instead of her."

"Thank you." Did everyone know I loved Coffee the most? Whatever. I didn't mind.

I dropped off my stuff, tugged anti-parasite booties and gloves on, grabbed the metal poop scoop, and headed for the airlocks.

My life: anti-parasite booties and poop scoops.

I laughed at myself until I stepped outside and saw Oliver.

He looked up when I made my way through the airlock. "Hey."

"Hey." I eyed the three fenced-in yards. Harvinder hadn't been kidding. All three of the fields were poop minefields.

"Do you mind helping me get this yard done first?" Oliver said. "So there's one for Harvinder to use?"

"Sure." Given Oliver outranked me, he didn't have to ask. He could just tell me what to do. But he always asked. It felt nicer to be asked. I started, emptying my scoop into the big rolling bin as I went, which was as gross as it sounded.

Every time I turned around, though, I caught Oliver watching me. After what felt like the tenth time of catching him staring, I couldn't handle it anymore.

"What?" I said, just as he said, "Beck?"

"Yeah?" I said, just as he said, "Sorry."

We stared at each other. Oliver blew out a noisy breath.

"Go ahead," I said, though I wasn't sure I wanted him to. No, scratch that. I *definitely* didn't want him to. He might be nice. And cute. But —

"I didn't know about you," Oliver said.

"What?" I didn't know what he meant.

"Mason never told me about you," Oliver said. "I know you two were a casual summer thing, but I want you to know I didn't know. About you and him, I mean."

"A casual summer thing." I swallowed. "Is that what he said?"

"Uh." Oliver blew out another breath. His face sort of crumpled, like he didn't want to repeat whatever Mason had really said.

Honestly? I knew I didn't want to hear it.

"Never mind." I put up one hand. I had no response beyond that. I mean, Mason made it perfectly clear he wanted me to stay away from Oliver. I'd been doing my best on that front. It felt like anything I could say would just piss Mason off more. And likely get me accused of crushing out again. "Okay, I have no idea what to say right now."

Oliver bit his bottom lip. "I broke up with him. Today. Just so you know."

"Oh." Well, fuck. School would be *delightful* tomorrow.

"It's just, there were things, and after what you said . . ." Oliver's crumple-face was back. "For the record? I'm sorry."

Okay, now I *really* had no idea what to say. "*You're* sorry?" I shook my head.

"I wouldn't have started seeing him if I knew about you," Oliver said, leaning on his poop scoop. "Even if you and he were casual." He shrugged, and then added, really quickly, like he wanted to make sure he hadn't said something wrong, "Nothing wrong with casual. It's just not really my thing."

"I didn't know we were casual," I said. Or, really, I blurted it. Like, it flew out of my mouth. "Which I know is on me, but he . . ." I shook my head. Ugh. This was gross.

"I get it." Oliver nodded. "Really."

Maybe he did.

I didn't have any more words left, so I got back to work, and he didn't speak, either. We got all three fields cleared, probably because we didn't talk beyond quick questions and answers about which field to clean next and who'd do what. When we were done, I leashed up Coffee, who jumped up at her kennel window when she saw me, making scolding *a-woo-woo-woo* noises, annoyed I'd taken so long.

Oliver walked Rosie and I walked Coffee. Coffee didn't fight our choice of direction like she used to. It helped I had a bag of treats in my pocket. She'd definitely realized she'd get cookies for sitting down at intersections.

"You're doing so well with her," Oliver said.

It broke the silence, and I jumped. I hoped he didn't notice.

He chuckled. "Sorry."

Yeah, he noticed.

"It's the treats," I said.

"Treats help," Oliver said. "But treats don't get

all the credit."

"I don't know," I said. "I mean, if someone offered me maple fudge, I'd be good."

He laughed and looked at me.

I shrugged. "It's my favourite." Why had I said that?

"I'm serious, though," Oliver said. "Coffee doesn't walk that well for me. Or Jonas."

"Well, she's the best dog ever," I said. Then I glanced at Rosie, who I swear paused long enough to glare at me. "No offence."

Rosie trotted on, totally turning her back on me.

"Too late. She's offended," Oliver said. "Rosie loves me best now."

I snorted.

We looped the field and came back to Rescues in Motion. I ran Coffee through the basic commands once more — *come*, *touch*, *sit*, and *down* — and she did all of them, grumbling the *entire* time she lay down. She *hated* doing *down*.

"So much attitude." I gave her the cookie.

She chomped it, and when I rubbed her behind her ear, she leaned into my hand and closed her eyes.

Oh wow. My chest clenched. Totally the best dog ever.

I spent longer than I needed to putting her back in her kennel, and she circled over and over again before settling on her dog bed and tucking her tail over her nose.

"See you later," I said.

When I turned to go, Oliver stood at the end of the kennel hallway, and his being there felt heavy. I walked up, and he was biting his bottom lip again.

"Do you have to be anywhere right now?" he said. "I've got my car, and I thought . . ."

I tried to make my face do something other than total panic at the thought of being alone with Oliver. I don't think it worked because he trailed off.

"I thought maybe we could talk," Oliver said. "Clear the air?"

My mom would love this guy, I thought randomly. *He likes communication*. Also, he'd been pretty damn good about everything. As much as I hated to admit it, Oliver did nothing wrong.

"I have to get back home," I said. Not at all true.

"Okay." Oliver had really dark brown eyes. Like puppy-dog eyes. "Another time?"

"Sure," I said, immediately regretting it.

Damn puppy-dog eyes.

We walked side-by-side to the bus stop, and he kept going, climbing into his car. I stared at my phone until he was gone.

A text popped up from Heather. **Check out the update**. She'd sent a link.

I tapped it. Heather hadn't been there today, but apparently, she'd worked on the website. Coffee's page loaded with the photo I'd taken of her running toward me instead of Jonas's awful one.

Heather definitely wrote the blurb.

Coffee is a northern blend who favours her husky side — she will talk, and she will give you sass — but had a rough start. She's hesitant around new people, and needs someone patient, gentle, and compassionate. She'll come to you when she's ready, especially if you have a treat to offer her, but once she's decided you're okay, be prepared for all the attitude.

I smiled. Heather went on to note the needs of a high-energy animal, and how she took longer with men, all with more of my photos mixed in. I went back to her text.

It's awesome, I wrote.

Patient, gentle, and compassionate – sound like anyone you know?

I laughed. Heather didn't do subtle.

Already told you, I can't.

I know, Heather's response came, and I could hear her voice doing that "told you so" thing. Just checking you weren't letting that shitty ex make you think you weren't those things.

Oh.

I smiled.

My bus was coming. I reacted to her text with a heart, and then climbed on to head home.

10 Today's Gay Agenda: TD&H

I SURVIVED WEDNESDAY AND THURSDAY without any face-to-face with Mason, but more than once I caught Amélie staring at me in Physics like I was something I'd scoop at Rescues in Motion. Nothing from Maya or A.J.

I saw Nico both days, but always with at least half the GSA group, Mason included, so I ate outside. I spent breaks in the library.

One hundred percent Coward Mode.

I drafted about a hundred texts to Nico, but decided I wanted a conversation in person, and instead checked in that we were still good for Friday.

Yep, he'd replied. **See you then.**

No emoji.

Oof.

Honestly, if not for Rescues in Motion, I'd have lost my mind. By Thursday, I had the dash from my locker to the bus stop down to an art, in the hope of catching the earliest possible bus and get to Rescues in Motion just after four, and not because my phone said it might rain.

On the bus, the stress of school and Mason and Nico faded away for another day. It would come back when I got up for school tomorrow, but for now, I'd take it.

At Rescues in Motion, I scooped poop, then took Coffee out into the yard for training.

"Come!" I pressed my fist to the centre of my chest.

Coffee tilted her head to one side, then trotted

toward me and sat down in front of me.

"Good girl!" I said, giving her the cookie. She chomped it down quickly, her bright blue eyes never leaving my face.

She knew exactly how many cookies I had.

"Down." I held my hand in the air.

She grumbled, took her sweet time as always, but she did lie down. The moment she got her treat, she was back up on her feet, though.

"Down is the worst, isn't it?"

That earned me an *a-woo-woo*.

"Sit." I curled my wrist.

She sat.

"Stay." I backed away from Coffee. She lowered her head, watching every step I took. I crossed the entire yard, and waited.

She kept her eyes locked on me. Her tail swished twice behind her. She might hate "down" but she *loved* this one.

I'd barely put my hand out to one side before she was in motion, racing toward me.

"Touch," I said, laughing, because she'd covered half the distance before I'd had the chance to say it. She skidded to a stop in front of me after tapping my open palm with her nose. I gave her a cookie, crouching down to rub her sides.

She leaned hard, knocking me over. I fell onto my butt and she pressed her head into my chest, so I gave her a big hug and scratches with both hands. Her tail whipped around like a helicopter blade.

"Who's amazing?" I said.

Coffee grumble-growled.

"Who's the best dog in the whole world?" I rubbed both sides of her face, flapping her ears. "Is it Coffee?"

She pressed one side against me, then the other, turning in circles so I could scratch her sides. She groaned when I found a good spot, her back leg kicking a bit in the air.

"It *is* Coffee!" I cheered. "Coffee is the greatest dog! In! The! World!"

Someone started clapping behind me, and I turned.

Oliver stood at the airlock. He grinned at me.

Okay, fine, totally fair. I got up off my butt and tried not to think about the baby-talk and cheering.

"Not a word," I said.

"I would never." Oliver held up both hands. "Harvinder and I dropped Buckley off at his new home and brought back a newbie. Want to meet him?"

"Buckley's gone?" That made two dogs finding a new place since I'd started here. Good for the grumpy little beagle. "I mean, sure." I eyed Coffee, and pulled the leash from my pocket. "You're not going to run away when I try to put your leash on, right? Best dog in the world, remember?"

Coffee eyed the leash then me. I swear she *grinned.* Her tail swished.

I reached for her. She ran off like a shot.

"Let me help," Oliver said, coming into the airlock.

Once Oliver got Coffee leashed, which only took two cookies this time, we went inside. The new arrival, a black lab with the *saddest* brown eyes ever, had two shaved IV spots in his fur on his front leg. I spotted another, larger shaved patch on his side. I could make out a long scar, but no stitches. His fur was growing back in.

"He had a run-in with a wild animal or another dog maybe," Oliver said. "Harvinder says he's fine for gentle exercise, though."

The dog just watched us from the bed, lying on his side. Poor guy looked miserable. The kennel smelled like vinegar from the really big clean in between dogs.

I hadn't done one of those yet. I wondered if I'd get taught.

"What's his name?" The little strip of painter's tape on the door still said "Buckley." Probably Harvinder hadn't had time to change it yet.

"Samson," Oliver said. "But I don't know if that's always been his name or if the vets gave it to him."

"Hi, Samson," I said.

No response. Samson's eyes stayed on us, but

nothing else.

"Let's see if we can get him out into a yard, at least." Oliver grabbed the leash from the hook and opened Samson's kennel.

Samson rolled over onto his stomach, but didn't get up, not even when Oliver put the leash on his collar.

"Hey, buddy," Oliver said. "You want to head outside? Maybe pee and have a little walk around before it rains?"

Samson lowered his head between his front paws.

"Aw," Oliver said. "You're killing me here."

"How do you feel about treats, Samson?" I pulled out a cookie.

Samson lifted his head, and licked his chops, but still didn't move.

"How about I just hold this here?" I kept my voice all light and easy. "I won't even look at you, okay?" I turned my head away. "See? No threat."

I heard Samson get to his feet, but I didn't look. He took the treat and ate it pretty much right out of my palm, though, without backing away. When I did look at him, he stared at me.

"This way," Oliver said, tugging gently on Samson's leash.

Samson allowed us to get him outside, and once we were through the airlock, he walked a slow circle around the edge of the yard, peeing against the fence a few times.

Oliver kept him on the leash, letting him explore at his own, slow pace. Samson's tail stayed low, but he started sniffing things, and Oliver fed him a few more treats and petted him.

A drop of rain hit my arm. I glanced up. "Here it comes."

"Let's get back inside, Samson," Oliver said. With a gentle tug, the black lab followed him back through the airlock.

By the time we had Samson back in his kennel, the rain picked up. We did our best to get each dog in and out to use the bathroom without getting us or the dogs drenched. Luckily, most were good about doing their business as fast as possible given the rain.

When my shift was over, I stood under the overhang at the front of Rescues in Motion. At least I could see the bus coming from there. I could run.

The door opened behind me, and Oliver came out.

"Want a ride home?" he said.

We'd had a good day today, but sharing a car ride with Oliver?

A roll of thunder made up my mind for me.

"You're sure?" I said.

Oliver just nodded, and pulled out his keys. We ran to his car, only getting slightly wet.

"What's your address?" Oliver asked, putting his phone into the little clip once we were inside. I gave it to him, and he pulled up his GPS. "That's pretty much on my way." He glanced at me.

His dark hair curled when it got wet, I noticed.

"Good," I said.

He smiled, and the puppy-dog eyes were back.

Cute. As always.

Oliver pulled out of the parking lot. I figured we'd drive in silence, other than the GPS.

"Are you coming on Sunday?" Oliver said. Rescues in Motion did monthly events where they brought the ready-to-be-homed dogs to parks or to other events where they could book space to try and find owners.

"I'm not scheduled," I said. "But my dad might be home. I'll bring him. He's allergic to dogs, but I want to show him what I've been doing."

"Might be home?" Oliver frowned.

"He's a truck driver," I said. "His schedule is rough."

"Ah."

More quiet.

"I saw your pictures," Oliver said. "They're really good."

For half a second, I thought he meant Today's Gay Agenda, and seriously panicked. Then I realized *of course* he meant the pictures of the dogs.

"Thank you," I said.

We stopped at a red light. Oliver tapped out a beat on his steering wheel, then laughed. "This is weird, right?"

"Yeah. And . . ." I needed to say something. "I'm sorry. I shouldn't have been so angry before. It wasn't your fault." I took a breath. "I felt really dumb. Which made me mad. Not your fault, though." I closed my mouth because I'd already said that.

The light turned green.

"You're not dumb," Oliver said. "For the record."

I snorted. "Well, apparently I have terrible taste in guys. Gaslighting assholes who ruin the word *adore*."

"Oh no." Oliver laughed a snort-bark of a laugh. "You, too? The forehead thing?"

I groaned, but Oliver grinned. Apparently, he thought it was funny.

Maybe it was?

"Well. At least the guys we date have great taste," Oliver said. "That's something."

"Too soon." But I laughed.

"Okay," Oliver said. The GPS interrupted, telling

him to turn, and Oliver followed its instructions. "But Mason clearly has a type."

I looked at him. "Gullible suckers?"

"No." Oliver shook his head. "Tall, dark, and handsome." He lifted his chin and smiled and somehow didn't come off arrogant. "I mean, look." He flicked one hand back and forth between us, including me.

"You are *way* cuter than me." The words were out before I could stop them, but *come on*. We both had dark hair and brown eyes, sure, and okay, yes, I'm tall, but Oliver had *great* shoulders, and I happened to know his chest had a sexy line of chest hair down the centre. I might be tall, but Oliver outclassed me in every other category.

"Dude," Oliver said. "No. You have dimples."

"Only people who don't have dimples like dimples." I happened to think my dimples made me look twelve years old.

He shook his head. "Nope."

The GPS told Oliver to turn onto my street and I

glanced up, pointing. "That's me, there."

Oliver pulled over. The sound of the rain on the windshield suddenly seemed really loud.

"Thanks for the ride," I said.

He nodded, then took a breath. "We're okay, right?"

"Yeah," I said, a little surprised. Because it felt like we were. I'd enjoyed the ride.

Huh.

"Okay," Oliver said. "Good. Here." He pulled his phone from the holder on his dashboard and handed it to me. "Put your number in. I'll let you know when I can give you rides home when we're on the volunteer schedule together. Most of my classes are in the morning."

Again, nice of him. I added myself. When I handed it back, he tapped on it before putting it back into the holder, and my phone vibrated in my pocket.

"Thanks again," I said, and got out of the car. I waved, and ran in the rain.

When I got inside, I checked the text he'd sent.

TD&H. It took me a second.

Tall, dark, and handsome.

I rolled my eyes, laughed, and added Oliver to my contacts.

11 Today's Gay Agenda: Eat Outside

NICO PULLED HIS OVERSIZED SUNGLASSES down his nose with one finger, staring at me over them. He'd painted his nails purple. Drama as always. "Bitch. It's been *years*."

"More like a couple of weeks," I said, feeling dumb just standing there in the field beside the school where I'd been eating my lunch all week. He dropped his messenger bag onto the grass and pulled me into a giant, tight hug.

I nearly burst into tears.

So. Clearly I was fine.

God, I'd missed him. When neither of us let go right away, my gut got all heavy and I needed to close my eyes for a second.

"Sorry," I said, which was funny because he also said "Sorry" at the same time. We both sounded kind of like we were choking.

We pulled back and stared at each other.

"Jinx?" His smile wasn't convincing.

"Let's sit," I said, and sat down. Otherwise, it felt like we'd stand there forever.

"This is ridiculous." Nico looked at me while I pulled my lunch out of my bag. "I do not eat outside. Why are we eating outside when we could be eating inside?" He glared at the grass, as offended as always that nature existed. "With our *friends*."

I stared at him. Did I really have to say it?

"Fine." He waved one hand and finally sat down, yanking his messenger bag open. "I get it." He pulled out his sandwich and took a bite, then lifted his phone and took a picture of me.

I raised one eyebrow.

"Proof of life for A.J.," he said, and I heard the little whoosh of him sending the photo off somewhere.

I laughed, but he stared at me.

Okay. So. This was fun. "How's Devon?"

"Do *not* with small talk," Nico said, rolling his eyes. "*What the fuck*, Beck? You *vanished*."

Ouch. Okay. "I didn't —" I started, but Nico's stare cut me right off. I blew out a breath. "Fine. Kind of?"

"Look," Nico said, tearing bits off his sandwich to eat. "I get you're upset and all. Mason said you —"

This time it was my turn to cut someone off. "Oh God. Can we not?" I held up my hand. "Mason is not my favourite topic right now."

"Right." Nico bit his lip. "Did you really take his phone?"

"What? Is that what he —?" I groaned, throwing my head back. "No! I saw a text from Oliver. Mason's phone was right there on the bed. It popped up on the screen."

Nico swallowed. "That's not what he said."

"Yeah, well, Mason isn't good at letting people know what's actually happening," I said. "Like, at all." I looked at Nico, but Nico looked anywhere but at my face. Oh no. "Wait. What *is* he saying? Is it bad?"

"Well, it's not great." Nico took a breath, like he had to work up to speaking. *Not great*? I braced myself. "He, uh, said you got clingy over summer."

I blinked. "Clingy."

"Like you wanted to date, didn't take it well when he turned you down . . ."

Turned me down?

"That's not . . ." I shook my head. "No. I never asked. *Not at all.*"

"Okay." Nico looked at me. "But you guys *did* have sex once?"

Once?

I rubbed my face with both hands, getting pissed. I so wasn't going to debate what counted as sex, but no way was it *once*.

"So that's a yes." Nico leaned against the wall.

"Not just once." I had to clear my throat.

"Oh." Nico frowned.

"Okay. To be clear? I thought we were boyfriends," I said. "I mean, we were hanging out all the time, and . . . having sex."

Nico frowned again. "Okay."

"Mason took the lead. I mean. You know me." I pointed at myself, and Nico slowly nodded but also didn't look entirely convinced.

That stung.

"Come on," I said. "Have I ever made the first move with any guy? Like, *ever*?"

"I guess not." Nico seemed to think that over. "No."

He sounded like he believed that at least. I'd take it. "I saw the text from Oliver." I blew out a breath. "I got upset. Mason was all, 'Beck, we never said we were dating.'"

"Oh." Nico wrapped his arms around his knees. He kept looking at me, though, like there was more, but he didn't want to say it.

"Oh God," I said. "What else?"

"I mean." Nico waved one hand to the side. "Okay. Did you really track down Oliver and tell him Mason cheated on you with him?"

"Did I *track down Oliver*?" I shook my head. "No! And you know that. I told you. Oliver volunteers at Rescues in Motion, too."

"You didn't know?" Nico said. "Before you signed up?"

What the hell? I couldn't believe Nico would ask me that. "Do you really think I'd do that?"

Nico shifted, putting his chin on his knees. He didn't say yes.

He also didn't say no.

"Wow," I said. Heaviness settled in my gut. "Does everyone think I'm some sort of stalker?"

"Beck, you just took off," Nico said. "I mean, you stopped coming to GSA, you didn't volunteer with us, nothing. You vanished. Mason didn't, and he said —" Nico sighed. "It looked bad, okay?"

"I didn't want to see Mason," I said. "He had me

convinced I was some sort of idiot for not understanding we were never a thing. And, fine, I was kind of an idiot, but it's not all on me." I pointed at Nico. "Even you told me to give him space, remember?"

Nico sighed. "True. But it didn't mean you had to ditch the rest of us."

"I didn't!" I said. Nico snorted, but now I was mad. I was so very done with other people telling me what I had and hadn't done.

Except, I had. Shit. I remembered my August photos. All-Mason, all-the-time.

"Okay," I said. "I did, over the summer. That was me. But not at school. Mason is always around the rest of you. I couldn't avoid *him* and also see everyone else. It sucks. I haven't seen you at school even *once* without Mason being there."

Nico flinched. "I guess."

"Amélie or Maya haven't said two words to me," I said. "Not even a text."

"You haven't texted them either, though," Nico said.

I hadn't. I sighed. We stared at each other.

He looked miserable. I definitely was.

"I'm not a stalker," I said. "I didn't track down Oliver to mess with Mason. Hell, I tried not to talk to Oliver, but he kept talking to me, and — okay, fine — yes, I told him I was with Mason in August. But Mason and I *were* together." I remembered how Heather put it. "I'm not a mind reader. He never used the word boyfriend, but he definitely didn't tell me I was just a fling. He said he *adored* me."

"Bitch, *really*?" Nico said, one eyebrow rising. "He said that?"

"*I adore you*," I said, pissed off all over again. "I take it that didn't make the Mason version of Beck the Stalking Psycho?"

Nico shook his head. "No."

"Well, he did." I sighed.

"Ew," Nico said.

"Right? I may not be sure of anything, but I know he said he adored me." God, I hated that word now. Mason had ruined it forever.

"You need to come back," Nico said. "To the GSA."

I laughed. "Seriously?"

"Beck —" Nico started, in his drama queen voice, but my phone pinged. A text from Heather popped up, and I saw Coffee's name, but I missed it. I tapped my phone back to life.

Any chance you can get here right after school? Before 4? Found a home for Coffee and they're coming today at 4. Thought you'd want to say goodbye.

I stared at the phone. I almost burst into tears right there. Someone was taking Coffee? *Today*? How could that be happening?

"What's wrong?" Nico said.

"I —" I had to clear my throat. "Someone's adopting Coffee."

Nico frowned, like he could tell this was a big deal, but didn't get *why*. "Isn't that good?"

I managed to nod, but I wanted to curl up in a ball. Even if my bus magically came early, I'd never make it in time. Normally I got there a little after four.

"Beck?"

"It's good." I choked on the words.

"Yet you look like you're going to have a breakdown."

"Because I'm going to have a breakdown." I swiped at my cheek. Crap.

"You're crying." Nico's voice caught. He always sympathy cried.

"Yep." I took a shaky breath. "Oh man. This sucks." I looked at my phone again. I couldn't get there on time. I needed to tell Heather.

"I'm sorry," Nico said.

"Thanks." I called up my texts, about to reply, but I noticed Oliver's text below Heather's. TD&H.

Oliver had a car.

He'd offered me rides.

This wasn't what he'd meant, but . . .

Before I could stop myself, I tapped his name.

Coffee found a home. Any chance you can get me to RIM before 4 to say goodbye?

"Beck?" Nico said. I glanced at him, and he

reached out and squeezed my shoulder. "You look awful."

"Thanks, bitch," I said, and Nico laughed. "But maybe this time I can do something about it."

I hit send, but the warning bell rang. Oliver hadn't replied by the time we had to go back to class.

The last three hours of the day sucked. I barely concentrated. The second the final bell rang, I ran. Right there on my phone was a reply from Oliver.

I'll meet you outside your school.

I threw everything into my bag and bolted, not even caring if people stared, though I slowed down to something not-quite-a-run whenever I saw teachers. I hit the doors and scanned the drop-off and pick-up area.

"Beck!"

Oliver's car was by the side of the road. He waved through the window, one arm visible above the roof of the car.

I jogged over and pulled open the door.

"Thank you." I pretty much collapsed into the

passenger seat.

"We'll be there in ten," Oliver said, pulling out into traffic.

I exhaled. My chest still felt like someone had tied a big knot in the centre of it, but we were on the way. I pulled out my phone and sent a text to Heather.

On my way.

Oliver told me. See you soon.

I looked at Oliver. Both hands on the wheel, his dark brown eyes scanning the road. I realized I had no idea where he'd been or what he'd been doing.

"I hope I didn't screw up your day," I said.

"You didn't," Oliver said. "In fact —"

He stopped. I looked at him. "What?"

"Nothing." He kept his eyes on the road. "We can talk later."

I stared out the window, wishing we could go faster.

12 Today's Gay Agenda: Say Goodbye

THE MOMENT I OPENED Coffee's kennel, I started snivelling, so when she came over and leaned against me, wagging her tail and happy to see me, I knelt down, buried my face in her fur, and tried not to be too loud.

"Good girl," I said, handing her a treat when I thought I wouldn't completely fall apart.

She crunched it happily and then lowered her head to look up at me with those incredible bright blue eyes. She grumble-growled, tapping one front paw on the tile floor.

"No, we're not going for a walk," I said. "I'm here to say goodbye."

My throat felt raw. My chest hurt. But Coffee wagged her tail and sat down in front of me, her big doggy grin in place. She tilted her head. I knew what was going through her brain.

I sat. Make with the cookie.

I gave her another treat.

Oliver crouched beside me, and I tried not to notice how close he was when he ruffled Coffee's ears with both hands. She let out one of her little growly-grumbles, and leaned against him while he scratched her side.

"Let's get her ready," Oliver said. He grabbed the leash from beside the kennel, which made Coffee's tail kick up to overtime. "Heather said we can use yard one."

"Okay." I sounded like I was choking.

Oh man.

Once we were in the yard, Coffee did zoomies, and I called her back to me with "come" and "touch" a few times, giving her treats and trying not to notice how fast time was going by. Oliver stood back and let me play with her.

I got her to sit, and then gave her another hug.

"You weren't supposed to break my heart," I said.

That got me an *awoo-woo-woo*, probably just because I had more treats in my hand. But maybe she was apologizing.

Coffee *was* pretty smart.

Then Heather came around the side of the building with what I guessed was a married couple — two women — and a little girl. The girl looked to be about ten, and she put her hands over her mouth and started crying the second she saw Coffee.

"She's so pretty!" More tears. "Oh!"

I could relate.

Coffee, for her part, had noticed their arrival and trotted over to stand between myself and Oliver, watching. Heather led the couple and kid through the airlock, and the first mom — who had more of a femme thing going on than the other — said, "Now remember, honey, it might take her a little while to get used to you."

"She's gotten much more confident, mostly thanks to these two." Heather nodded to Oliver and me. "But your mom is right. Coffee might not want to play right away."

"Do you want to give her a treat?" Oliver said.

"Hold it on your hand," the other mom said. "Nice and flat."

The little girl nodded. Oliver handed her a cookie. Coffee watched intently, and when the little girl held out her hand, Coffee didn't hesitate. She stepped right up and licked the cookie right off.

The girl squealed in delight.

Which made Coffee grumble-growl at her.

The girl stopped squealing and stared at Coffee in utter joy.

"She likes to talk," I said. I had to clear my throat after.

"A-woo-woo-woo!" the girl said, trying to deepen her voice.

Coffee grumble-growled right back, wagging her tail.

"Okay, let's go over all her paperwork, and then you three can take her home." Heather reached down and attached a new leash to Coffee's collar. Heather glanced at me.

I took a deep breath and nodded. I even managed a smile.

The family, and Coffee, left through the airlock together. Coffee glanced back at me once, tail wagging, as they went through the door, and that was it.

The moment the door closed behind them, I turned around and lost it.

Okay, Beck. Get it together.

I wiped my face and took a deep breath. Coffee was going to go to a new home to have a great life. She'd been rescued, literally the point of Rescues in

Motion. It was right there in the name and everything. I'd known that going in. Today was a good day.

Nope.

Today fucking *sucked.*

Also, I'd just sobbed my ass off with Oliver less than ten steps away. I mean, I'd turned my back, and he hadn't said anything, but no way he didn't notice.

So embarrassing.

I turned around.

Oliver had his back to me. For a second, I wondered if he'd been sniffling, too, but then I noticed he had his hand out beside him, palm up and . . .

I stared at the little brown square in his palm. Not a dog treat.

"Is that fudge?" I swiped at my cheek.

"Yes," he said. I could tell he was smiling even though he had his back to me.

"What are you doing?"

"Trying to get you to trust me," Oliver said. "So, no eye contact. Hand to the side. Treat."

I laughed. It was a shaky laugh, and felt weird

after crying, but it also felt good.

Oliver didn't move.

He was being funny, right?

"You bought fudge?"

"You said it was your favourite." He still hadn't turned, still had his hand out. Not looking at me.

This was ridiculous. I wasn't a shy dog.

"Oh my God, turn around!"

Oliver finally turned around, and maybe I should have made him keep his dark brown eyes aimed somewhere else, because wow. The way he looked at me made me feel exposed, or on display, or something I couldn't quite put my finger on.

Oliver wasn't just looking at me. Oliver saw me. That's what it felt like.

"I like you," Oliver said.

"What?"

"I like you, Beck." He smiled. "You're pretty great."

I had no idea what to say. Oliver thought I was pretty great? Oliver liked me? It didn't seem possible.

He got you here in time to say goodbye to Coffee.

That was a pretty big deal. Also, no denying the fudge. It was literally right there. He brought me candy.

He said he liked me.

And man, the way he was looking at me right now? Yeah, no wonder dogs preferred grabbing treats from our hands while we couldn't see them.

Speaking of . . .

"I'm not going to eat fudge out of your hand." I cleared my throat. I held my own hand out, and he smiled, then gave me the little square of fudge.

"I didn't think you would." He kept watching me, and I had absolutely no idea what to say. Also, the fudge was melting.

"Uh-huh," I said. Then — because what the hell else could I do? — I bit the fudge. Maple flavour spread over my tongue. I blinked in amazement.

The exact kind I'd said was my favourite.

He remembered.

"We okay?" Oliver took a step closer to me. His

smile was tugging up on one side more than the other, and I'd bet he was trying not to laugh. "You're not going to bolt?"

"I mean, you gave me fudge. Could be time for zoomies." I shrugged. "But, we're fenced in. I can't run away. The airlock is in the way."

That made him laugh, which is what I'd wanted, but then he got all serious again. And serious looked really good on Oliver. Like, his eyes were doing that "I see you" thing again. He took a deep breath. "I mean it. I like you."

I ate the last of the little square of fudge for courage. "Oliver," I said, and then I didn't really know where to go. Because if I was being honest with myself, maybe I liked him, too, but —

But. But what?

"I won't break your heart." Oliver shrugged when I raised one eyebrow. "I heard what you said to Coffee."

Right. That. But that. Exactly that.

"I mean, Coffee just showed me that's a promise

no one can keep," I said. "Not even dogs."

"Well," Oliver said. "How about a date? And it would be a date." He smiled. "If dates go well, we can try being boyfriends. I promise to be very clear at every step."

Okay, well, that was kind of the best possible thing he could say, ever.

"My mom is going to love you," I said.

He laughed. "Not who I'm trying to impress here, Beck."

"Yeah, but the whole communication thing?" I waved a hand back and forth, teasing. "That's good."

"How good?" he asked. He took another step forward, and now he was right in front of me. "Just so I know how I'm doing."

Oliver really was TD&H. Dark brown eyes. Great chin. And those shoulders. But how kind he'd been, teaching me things? His way with dogs? The ride here, the fudge, the promise to be honest and clear?

Those blew nice eyes and chins and shoulders right out of the water.

I leaned forward, and he met me halfway. He leaned into the kiss, letting me take the lead which was terrifying but also fun, and when I let my tongue explore a bit, he pulled one arm around my shoulders.

Our first kiss tasted like maple fudge. Maple fudge had just become something totally Oliver for the rest of my life.

Eventually, I pulled back, though I didn't really want to.

"Very good," I said. "How you're doing, I mean."

Oliver grinned.

I took a big breath.

"You okay?" he said.

"Oh, y'know," I laughed. "All my friends are mad at me, but I talked to my best friend. Only, from him I found out what Mason told everyone. Then a dog broke my heart. But I kissed this really hot guy . . ." He grinned again when I got to that last part. "Today's been sort of a . . . whole journey."

"Sounds rough," he said.

"He brought me maple fudge though," I said.

"And asked me out."

"Yeah, he did," Oliver said. "But you didn't answer him."

"Yes," I said.

"Yes . . . ?"

"Yes, a date." I smiled.

He grinned again. I really liked his grin. Then he got serious again. "What did Mason tell your friends?"

"I'm a stalker, basically?" I shook my head. "Clingy and neurotic? And I avoided them, so they only got his version of the story, and . . . that's my fault."

"Ow."

"Yeah."

Oliver took my hand and squeezed it. "What are you going to do?"

Good question.

13 Today's Gay Agenda: Be Seen

We're on our way. Nico's text pinged.

I tried not to throw up.

"I hate this." I turned my mug around on the top of the table.

"It'll be okay." Oliver bumped his shoulder against mine. The coffee shop wasn't particularly busy, so we'd managed to grab the big corner booth at the back. The place was close enough to Bruce House that it wouldn't take my friends long to get here.

Assuming I could still call them my friends.

We're on our way. "We" meant it wasn't just Nico. That meant something, right?

I took a deep breath. My dad's schedule hadn't worked out after all, and he wouldn't get home until late tonight, so I'd spent the day with Oliver at the Patterson Park event for Rescues in Motion, all three hours. Because I wasn't officially there to volunteer, I made it my own goal to take pictures of all the dogs while Oliver collected information from people who might be able to give dogs temporary homes. In between me taking photos and him getting people to fill in forms on clipboards, we'd hung out.

Being with Oliver felt nothing like being with Mason, who'd only wanted to be together when we were alone. Oliver put his arm around me when he was on his break, and he kissed me before he went back to his clipboard.

Not on my forehead.

And he'd come with me to the coffee shop, once he'd learned Nico had agreed to bring the GSA group here after Bruce House.

Meeting everyone seemed like such a good idea when I'd been texting Nico yesterday. Of course, yesterday night Oliver and I had gone out to see a movie, and so I was riding an Oliver high.

He even met my mom.

I looked at Oliver, and he smiled. The high came back. "It'll be okay."

I tried to believe it. I scrolled through photos while we waited.

"Pretty sure those are going to clear the kennels," Oliver said, nodding back at the phone screen. I'd caught Samson the black lab in the middle of shaking his head. His big dopey grin — not to mention floppy ears — made him look like the giant goofball he was. Probably my favourite shot of the day. I swiped to the next photo, Chopper, who I'd photographed rolling on his back. The big yellow dog had thrown himself onto his back every time someone came near him, begging for belly rubs. I'd gotten right up to his face, and you could see his tiny front teeth, which made him look like he was smiling.

"I bet Chopper is the next to get a new home," I said. "He's a lot, but no one could resist the belly rubs."

"Okay," Oliver said, taking my phone and scrolling back a few shots until he got to Cinnamon. "I pick her." The red-brown mutt had been looking at squirrels in a tree, and I'd caught her all alert and focused, head tilted. "She's a sweetheart, and people loved her." He scrolled a few more photos. "You're so good at this." He kept going, and I let him, enjoying watching him react to the pictures. Then he paused, and I realized he'd gotten to the picture of Coffee I'd cropped for Today's Gay Agenda the day she'd gone home with her new family.

"Aw," he said. "That's a great shot. Was this on our site?"

"No. It was for this feed I have," I said. I'd never told anyone about Today's Gay Agenda before. But because it was Oliver — and Coffee — I wanted to explain. "I post one photo, every day."

"Cool." He smiled. "Can I see?"

I sucked in a breath, and he frowned. "What?"

"I've never shown anyone before," I said. "I mean, people follow it — more people than follow my account — but no one knows it's me."

"If you don't want to —" he started.

"No." Now that I'd said it out loud, I really wanted to show him. I picked up my phone and pulled up the feed, handing it back to him. I watched him looking, and he got this little smile on his face.

"Every day it's one photo, and what's on the agenda," I said. "It's a joke, I guess, pointing out how the whole idea of some massive Gay Agenda is dumb."

"Say Goodbye," he said, reading the caption of the picture of Coffee. Then he scrolled back further. He chuckled at "Doubt," which was another picture of Coffee, and laughed out loud at "Don't Get Parasites," with the poop scoops, boot coverings, and gloves.

"How do you pick what you post for the day?" He kept scrolling.

"Depends on the day," I said. "Sometimes something really stands out, but sometimes it's something silly like 'Don't Get Parasites.'"

"Anything stand out today?" Oliver looked up, doing that playful smile thing he could do.

Man, he was cute.

"You," I said. It was the truth. Today had been amazing, and so simple. He'd so obviously been *with* me today. Also, he'd introduced me as his boyfriend, *twice*, when two of his friends had shown up.

"How about us?" Oliver said, handing me my phone and leaning against my shoulder.

I framed us in a selfie, giving myself lots of room to play with, and spent a few minutes cropping it. Once I was happy with where we ended up — our heads were in the top-left of the shot, the brown seat behind us really making Oliver's dark brown eyes stand out — I showed it to him.

He smiled. "Definitely my agenda."

I paused. I'd never put anything obviously *me* on Today's Gay Agenda before. But after today . . .

I uploaded the photo. After a second thinking, I wrote the caption.

Today's Gay Agenda: Be Seen.

Oliver smiled.

I hit post, and that was that. It was out there. Oliver and me.

It felt *great.*

The door opened, and I heard Nico's voice before I saw him. Maya and Amélie were with him, and A.J. waved as they all went to get in line.

No Mason.

"Here we go," I said, waving back. Oliver squeezed me, and I realized he hadn't pulled his arm away. There was no mistaking how we were sitting together.

Be Seen. It really did feel great. But there was more on the agenda today. Oliver couldn't be the whole shot, every day. We waited while everyone got their drinks, and they came over. Nico led the way, sliding into the booth.

"Hey, Beck," Nico said, pulling his sunglasses down his nose and pointedly looking at Oliver's arm around my shoulders. "And nice to see you again, Oliver."

"Hi," Oliver said, grinning right back at him.

Maya and Amélie weren't quite as comfortable, I could tell, but that was fair. I knew they'd only had Mason's version of the story.

"Hey," I said to them. "Thanks for coming."

"Hi," Maya said.

Amélie nodded, and said, "Sure."

It got quiet, and awkward, and A.J. cleared their throat. "So . . ." they said, waving one hand in front of Oliver.

Right. I looked at my friends. I'd done *Be Seen.*

Time for *Be Heard.*

"So," I started, and my voice sort of cracked. Oliver took my hand and squeezed it. That helped. I tried again. This time, I sounded like me. "The reason I stopped coming to GSA wasn't what you think, and I want you to know what really happened."

It took over an hour. They had questions, and I did my best to answer them, though sometimes the honest answer was "I don't know." Oliver backed up the parts he could, and made it really clear that neither of us had known about each other when we'd started seeing Mason.

Also, at one point A.J. pointed back and forth between us and said, "So, are you two, like . . . ?" and Oliver said, "We're boyfriends."

I kind of lost a few minutes after that. Boyfriends. After everything with Mason, hearing Oliver use the word with our friends meant everything.

Eventually, though, our conversation wound down and of course it was Nico who asked the biggest question of the whole thing.

"Why didn't you just tell us?" Nico shook his head, like he still couldn't understand that part, even after everything I'd explained.

They were all looking at me. A.J., Maya, and Amélie. Nico.

I almost said "I don't know" again, and truthfully, I'm not sure I'd ever know why my first instinct had been to run away, but I did know some of it now.

"I felt really pathetic," I said. "And dumb. When Mason said I shouldn't have assumed we were together,

I started second-guessing myself."

Nico frowned, and I held up my hand to stop him from saying anything yet.

"It's not all on Mason. It really isn't," I said. "I mean, he was awful, don't get me wrong, but I didn't even try to reach out to any of you, and that's my fault. I took off. I made it easy for him to gaslight you as much as he was gaslighting me, and . . . I'm sorry about that."

Oliver squeezed my hand again.

A.J. let out this massive sigh. Nico nodded. Maya and Amélie both looked down. Maya, especially, looked really upset, and I think it was the kind of upset I was feeling, too: upset with herself.

"What an asshole," A.J. said. I'd never heard them sound mad before, but they sounded mad now. Everyone looked at them, and they lifted their shoulder. "Mason. Seriously."

"Right?" Nico said.

I let out a big sigh of my own. "I really am sorry," I said.

"Us too," Maya said. Amélie nodded.

"It kind of sucks not having you at Bruce House," Nico said. I could have hugged him for changing the subject. "I think you'd really like it there."

"You really would," Maya said. "We're getting all these great stories and stuff."

"Did you know the whole reason our Pride is in August is because there was a whole massive protest in August, back in the seventies?" A.J. said, leaning forward. "I had no idea. I figured it was just because Toronto is bigger, and they didn't want to overlap."

"Really?" I blinked. "Huh. That's cool."

"You can't have him," Oliver said, shaking his head and tapping the table with his free hand. "He's doing amazing at Rescues in Motion. He's a dog-whisperer. You're not taking him." He paused, and tugged me in for a quick kiss. "He's mine."

Yeah, okay, I was never going to get tired of that.

Nico lifted his hands, laughing. "Understood."

"Is it fun?" A.J. asked. "Working with dogs?"

"It's awesome," I said. "Except for one part. But it's worth it."

"What?" Maya said, frowning. "What part?"

I pulled out my phone and scrolled back to the first picture I ever took of Coffee. "Let me tell you all about this one dog," I said. I put my phone out where they could all see her, and the whole group made "aww!" sounds.

"This is Coffee," I said. "She broke my heart." I smiled at Oliver, who smiled right back. "But it's okay. I got better."

ACKNOWLEDGEMENTS

I owe a big thank-you to Becky Cochrane, who is both a wonderful author and editor I've worked with in the past, and also a force of nature when it comes to rescue animals. She answered all my poop and non-poop questions, and any mistakes left over in the story about running rescues are totally my own. Also, major credit goes once again to my editor, Allister, who continues to be a champion as well as offering real insight. I've said it before, and I'll say it again: editors don't get enough credit for the work they do, especially given how much they make our words shine. Last, but never least, thank you to my husband, Dan, who pointed out everyone loves a dog and my idea would work better with a dog (he was right), and also to Max the Husky, who doesn't wait anymore for me to turn away before he goes for whatever treat is at hand. Don't break my heart for many, many more years, okay?

Québec, Canada